KINETIC SOLUTIONS

A HANDSOME ROB GIG

BLAZE WARD

KNOTTED ROAD PRESS

Kinetic Solutions
A Handsome Rob Gig
Blaze Ward
Copyright © 2022 Blaze Ward
All rights reserved
Published by Knotted Road Press
www.KnottedRoadPress.com

ISBN: 978-1-64470-277-2

Cover art:
Illustration 11697350 / Alien © SpinningAngel | Dreamstime.com

Cover and interior design copyright © 2022 Knotted Road Press

Reviews
It's true. Reviews help. Even a short one, such as, "Loved it!" So please consider reviewing this book (and all of the ones you've read) on your favorite retailer site.

Never miss a release!
If you'd like to be notified of new releases, sign up for my newsletter.

http://www.blazeward.com/newsletter/

Buy More!
Did you know that you can buy directly from my website?

https://www.blazeward.com/shop/

ALSO BY BLAZE WARD

First Centurion Kosnett

Encounter at Vilahana

Consensus at Aditi

Hegemony at Dalou

Princes at Ewin

Empire at Gloran

Domain at Yaumgan

The Jessica Keller Chronicles

Auberon

Queen of the Pirates

Last of the Immortals

Goddess of War

Flight of the Blackbird

The Red Admiral

St. Legier

Winterhome

Petron

CS-405

Queen Anne's Revenge

Packmule

Persephone

Shadow of the Dominion

Longshot Hypothesis

Hard Bargain

Outermost

Dominion-427

Phoenix

Princess Rualoh

The Handsome Rob Gigs

Can't Shoot Straight Gang

Can't Shoot Straight Gang Returns

Hunting Handsome Rob

Handsome Rob, Assassin

Kinetic Solutions

Earth Force Sky Patrol

Birth of the Star Dragon

Flight of the Star Dragon

Call of the Star Dragon

Shadow of the Star Dragon

Trial of the Star Dragon

Hunter Bureau

Mirrors

Latency

Fairchild

Fairchild

Strawberry Dragon

1

HIS IDENTITY PAPERWORK SAID ROBERTO SEGURA. SIX-foot-one. One-ninety-five. Black eyes. Black hair. Hispanic genotype. At least the last five were accurate. And his beloved mother remained at home seventy-five light-years away, so nobody was likely to hear him called by any other name around here.

That was good, since any other name would likely get him killed. Especially with the sorts of folks he was playing with these days.

These days, most people called him *Handsome Rob*.

Once upon a time, he'd been a mere Courier, after retiring from the *Lincolnshire* Navy. Then a Field Agent for the *Lincolnshire Guardia Civil Interior*.

The Service.

From there, he'd made the step up to Assassin. Top of the pay and prestige scale, as long as he was in the field. Sure, he had bosses back home. Civil servants and political appointees. Some of them had even previously served in the field, doing what he had done. A few, anyway.

Precious few assassins stayed in the game long after they

reached the age where they couldn't handle the brutal physicality of things. Too many ways to get hurt. To get killed.

Lots of unfriendly folks out there. People with an ax to grind. A score to settle. Sometimes, it was personal. Most of the time the bullet with your name on it was addressed to *Dear Occupant*.

Like today.

They say that after long enough, you just develop that ninth sense, the one that tells you someone has a high-powered rifle with a telescopic, gyro-stabilized, ballistic computer attached, waiting for you to step into the killing zone so they can maintain plausible deniability later when a literal bolt from the blue strikes you down for having made one or more of the gods angry.

Handsome Rob had felt that itch more than once. Ducking and running for no reason he could explain had probably kept him alive.

Today, the shoe was on the other foot. He had the rifle. And all the accessories that both the agency and a few civilian friends had been able to dream up, given budget, need, and craziness.

Today felt crazy.

Weather overhead was a stable, cool marine layer, so the air would remain heavy and wet until it burned off later. That would make the timing of the shot tricky, because the bullet would be in the air for so long. No breeze at present, but again, heat would cause things to stir later.

He was sitting behind a rock just under a mile from his target, covered with a cloak that automatically adjusted its color and texture to the terrain around the edges. Basically, the whole thing was a giant picture frame that could display whatever image you wanted.

Today, he was a boulder.

You were supposed to do things like this with a partner, as well. Someone to watch your butt while you were focused on a target. To shoot at anyone trying to creep up on you while you were crept up on someone else.

Security around Rob's target was too good. Rob had been able to manage the sneak, but there were a handful of folks he knew good enough. Plus, every body that came along added to the chance that someone would see or hear something. Perhaps trip an eyebeam and turn on a trail camera.

Something.

At this distance, he was using bullets rather than beams. Any beam emitter capable of killing a man from this far out in this weather would have been exceptionally bulky and heavy. And likely contained enough electronics and metal to set off a passive scanner somewhere.

Handsome Rob was stripped down about as far as he could get, relying on stuff so primitive that modern defenses probably didn't think about it. He would show on many scanners as a deer or bear by mass, and there were enough of those running around these woods that you couldn't rely on machines.

He had no radio. No electronic transmitters at all. Even his spotting scope was entirely glass, though precisely polished and tuned by experts. He didn't use a distancing laser here, relying on extremely detailed paper maps and a little geometry to go with a manual computer not much more sophisticated than an abacus.

Somewhere, Mr. Hobson was laughing, after an eighth-grade Rob had snapped his fingers and asked when the man thought he might need geometry in his adult life.

The scope had been selected for the range, dialed in to zero before Rob had set out, once the parameters of the mission had come into shape. One shot. Extreme range. Get out safely.

Helped that his target had chosen to build his vacation dacha on the side of a mountain, one overlooking a spectacular view of a river valley below them. Wide patio faced the view, a slab of concrete with a three-foot barrier all the way around like a castle wall. Keep folks from accidentally sliding down the side of a mountain.

Here, it meant that Rob had a clear view across the valley, slightly downhill from where he was currently hidden and waiting.

You generally didn't want to rely on someone else being precise about their daily habits, but the gentleman over there was known to emerge from the rest of the big manor house at around eleven thirty on the local clock, having been up since before dawn in the summer.

Dude was one of those weirdos who operated on four to five hours of sleep and had been like that for as long as the Service had records or rumors about the man.

Rob checked the time on the display inside his spotting lenses. 11:26. Big, binocular vision let him see a wider field of view than the shooting scope on his rifle. Table set for two, as the reports had suggested.

The old man would be facing out. Not quite square on to Rob, but only around seventeen degrees slant. By design. The table could hold six, but only two chairs and a tablecloth were set today, the white linen of the cloth still and heavy, which would let Rob account for any breeze over there.

None. Good.

Fancy plates and crystal had been set out, along with a reading tablet no doubt connected to the house network and secured against electronic intrusion. Coffee service off to one side. The owner liked fresh cream and brown sugar in his coffee, but made allowances for strangers with weird habits, from the other options on the silver serving tray.

Through the plate glass windows and doors leading inside, Rob could see shadowed movement. The stuff wasn't glass, but a complex polymer that would stop anything short of an anti-aircraft missile, even instantly polarizing to reject a laser touching it.

But for his need to sit in the sun on a nice day and have lunch, the man would be impregnable in there.

Which would play to his ego. As intended.

He had a guest today. A possible recruit looking to gain access to his organization. A dangerous outsider who could turn into a mole if allowed, burrowing in and causing all sorts of havoc later, when nobody was looking.

That was why the Service had tapped Handsome Rob to be here today. This needed to look good.

Three men emerged from the interior, the head butler escorting Rob's two targets to the table while holding a carafe of fresh coffee in one hand. There was already a pitcher of iced water in place. Ultrasonics would keep the bugs at bay, so the butter was room temperature and safe.

Rob could almost smell the freshly baked sourdough bread that would be served shortly.

The two men sat, with the lord of the manor facing out and the visitor turned away from Rob. Again, not quite on a line.

Handsome took one quick look around his own location, then put his binoculars away and picked up the rifle. Good, old-fashioned maple wood. Heavy and sturdy. The kind of thing you wanted in a rifle with this kind of range.

The barrel was longer than commercial versions, a custom model the factory manufactured for long-range hunters and the Service under the table. Bipod on the front stabilized things. Bolt action for a right-handed shooter, to keep the number of moving parts to a dead minimum and allow them to be manufactured to nearly impossible tolerances. Just as the bullets were specially loaded to go with the shot this morning.

Necessary when engaging at a range of about fifteen hundred yards on a nice day.

Rob cycled the bolt open just enough to confirm that the weapon was loaded. It was a well-trained habit in a shooter. Every gun was loaded, even when you had confirmed that it was not.

Magazine would hold three more rounds, but Rob didn't foresee needing a second shot.

He was only here to create chaos today.

Even as an assassin, the number of people he'd actually killed was currently the lowest ever recorded by the Service.

Rob preferred social assassination, whenever possible. You could destroy someone without ever hurting them physically.

He was rather better at that than anybody else currently employed in his division.

Today, he had two targets when the butler withdrew. Two men facing each other across a nice table, chatting about something in the manner of relative strangers establishing a basis for friendship. Or at least networking.

Rob doubted that they would ever be friends. You didn't have friends in this line of work. You had acquaintances and co-workers. Plus enemies who may and may not have real names.

Or just codenames by which folks knew them.

Sometimes, you weren't a man anymore. Just a number in a file.

Nature of the business.

Rob confirmed that nobody else was on the patio then

started blocking out everything around him as he put his eye to the scope.

The lord of the manor didn't like ties. He wore his white shirt buttoned to an open collar under a snazzy sportscoat blazer. Gray today right on the edge of steel blue. Middle-aged man. Not as red-brown as Rob's skin, but not as pale as you might encounter in places like *Fribourg*.

He was too far away to see, but the file said hazel eyes, boring in on his visitor as they talked. Rob didn't bother reading lips, as nothing consequential would be said. Two men, strangers at a bar if you will, chatting.

Rob shifted down a bit to the visitor. Male. Younger. Not as young as Rob's twenty-nine years, but not much beyond it. Dressed just as formally, with the addition of a tie, invisible now but a muted blue with green stripes when he'd been walking out to the table.

Rob flipped off the rifle's safety and concentrated on his breathing.

The waiter returned with the bread bowl. Rob couldn't help his mouth watering as he watched steam rise off the cloth covering it. Rumor on the street said it was fantastic sourdough, a starter culture over a century old at this point. Those same rumors said that the man had paid a staggering amount of money for it, from the sorts of collectors who maintained those types of breeding programs.

Lunch would be along shortly, but for now, the men enjoyed coffee and freshly baked bread, oblivious to the angel of death just over the visitor's shoulder with a rifle in hand.

In the most primitive era, you fired a thing made up of a brass shell filled with gunpowder that was ignited at the base. The burning powder created pressure, forcing the bullet itself forward up a sealed tube of a barrel, grooved with rifling to impart spin and help with accuracy at range.

These days, the physics was similar, but the execution was vastly different.

The casing had a small charge at the bottom that lit, but it was little more than a jolt to push things to the end of the barrel. Lower pressures were needed, because the middle of the casing was a small rocket that was fired only after the bullet and solid-fuel part had cleared the barrel, spinning madly and centered.

Then the rocket would light, and the bullet would continue to accelerate for about three hundred yards, hitting a little above Mach three at the peak before starting to slow down again.

If you needed to kill an unarmored vehicle, you could put a heavy bullet with a tip designed to punch clean holes in things. To kill a man, you used something softer, so that it would rupture immediately on impact, shredding things as it spalled off fragments.

Most of the time, hunters used a slug about midway between the two, so that the bullet might not be neutralized passing through undergrowth or hitting bone. An elk almost never died immediately, but succumbed to the blood loss from a hole through its chest.

Men were no different, and the lord of the manor over there had a top-notch medical suite and trained staff on hand at all times. More prepared for poison or heart attack, but Rob assumed a competent trauma surgeon with the amount of money on the table.

Movement at the door and Rob smiled. He caught feet coming into his view. Nice shoes. Expensive slacks. Top lieutenant of the lord, coming to discuss something.

The third man moved right next to the boss and everything came to perfect rest.

Rob breathed out and pulled the trigger as the underling

leaned in to whisper some important message having to do with a phone call that had just come in.

Right on time.

The impact on Rob's shoulder was that smooth, hard jolt he'd trained for. Everything felt just right, so he didn't bother racking another round and instead focused on the image in the scope.

The bullet itself had been moving too fast to actually see, even watching right down the flight line. It was more like the after-strobe of a lightning bolt in his retina. Even the rocket section didn't generate smoke, a design feature to keep someone from following the trail back to the shooter when they might have heavy weapons they could use to just hose an area ddown. Instead a simple *crack* as it went supersonic.

Rob remained perfectly still.

The flunky was down. Worse, Rob's shot had caught him sideways in the ass, right through the fleshly parts in a way that would be amazingly painful, forever to heal, and almost no risk of actually killing the man.

As intended.

Image was everything in this game. Even when you needed a distraction.

Handsome Rob smiled as all hell broke loose on the patio over there and everyone scrambled madly to get under cover by sliding their butts up against that concrete retaining wall, down and out of sight.

Gunmen poured out of the house itself, aiming every which way. One of them began to yell and presumably the doctor was being summoned for the most embarrassing wound a man might survive.

Still, ballistics would eventually track the shot backwards and determine that it had come just over the shoulder of the man sitting with his back to the valley.

He would even be able to say he'd felt it pass. Probably

smelled it, though everybody would smell the residue and some of them would know the scent.

Someone had taken a shot at the visitor and missed.

As intended.

Elsewhere, rumors were being circulated that the Service had tried to kill the man. Almost true, too.

The visitor must indeed be a serious criminal if the Service was sending assassins after him. And a powerful and dangerous one, at that. The lord of the manor would see the importance of going into business with the stranger.

Who would then learn everything he needed to know about the organization so he could file a report much later and have everyone arrested.

Not every assassin killed people, after all. Sometimes, it was the full organization he was after.

Handsome Rob smiled and began packing his gear.

Mission accomplished.

2

MIGUEL ELLIOT CABRILL WAS A STOUT, BALD, GRAY MAN. Exceptionally tall, which was the only thing memorable about him in a job that required him to maintain a low profile, most of the time.

His desk was almost a castle with fortifications, as various piles of files and dockets were stacked with the edges, perfectly aligned, crenelated across the front of his desk and installed vertically behind him on the credenza.

Today, he couldn't help his fidgets. He reached out a hand to key the intercom to Robin, his executive assistant.

"Where is he now?" Miguel asked simply.

"Last report had him flirting with the cute redhead at the coffee shop, sir," Robin replied with a grin in his voice.

"She's one of ours, right?" Miguel demanded.

"Deep cover, Director," Robin assured him. "Set up for triple-plays as necessary."

Miguel grunted and released the button. The whole system was internal, with wires because any radio signal could be intercepted. The Service kept its headquarters as secure as possible.

That included recruiting cute redheads at nearby coffee shops to keep watch for any potential enemy agents paying too much attention to Miguel's own staff when they went for a quick jaunt.

The intercom beeped again. Miguel pressed it.

"Visual confirmation that he has left the coffee shop finally and is headed this way," Robin said.

"Good," Miguel replied. "Send Ben in now and Handsome when he arrives."

Ben Sevier had been Miguel's executive assistant prior to Robin Hill, before being promoted to Chief of Staff. Head of the paperwork section of the entire building in more ways than one, though few people actually reported to the man directly.

The door opened and Ben stepped in. He was tall and still athletic but starting to get squishy around the middle as he got into his later thirties. Short brown hair and green eyes that didn't miss anything.

Useful, as Miguel was still cleaning up the mess left by the arrest and subsequent execution of Stansfield Brightmeadow-Gates, Ben's predecessor in the role who had gone rogue and tried to have Handsome Rob killed to get back at the folks Brightmeadow-Gates had derisively referred to as the *Cowboys on Three*.

Field Operations. Folks like Rob and his semi-retired, semi-informal mentors: the *Can't Shoot Straight Gang*.

Old rivalries and hatreds that had gotten out of hand.

"Sit," Miguel instructed Ben, pointing to the chair on the left.

Ben had seen the delivery this morning, but it had been marked Eyes-Only-Director, so he hadn't read the contents. Miguel had, and had set in motion a chain of events that included Handsome Rob flirting with baristas because

Miguel had been unwilling to sound enough of an alert to bring the man running.

Others would be watching the building. Would react to a higher state of vigilance and react themselves. That was to be avoided whenever possible.

Espionage, contrary to public opinion and mass media, was a quiet, deliberate thing, taking years to assemble small clues and disparate bits of data into information.

Except when it wasn't, and you had to rely on wild cards like Roberto Segura. Handsome Rob as trained and polished by no less than Jorge Royo, the supposedly washed up, third-rate-actor best known for a series of comical farce vids that happened to make pretty good money, and let Royo and the rest of the *Can't Shoot Straight Gang* occasionally perform missions for the Service.

When all else had failed.

Miguel was just hoping that Handsome Rob alone would be sufficient. One of these days, somebody would figure out Royo's real game, martini glass and seduction of available women notwithstanding.

Robin knocked at the door, opened it far enough, and ushered Handsome in before closing it.

"Sit," Miguel ordered the agent, one of his current favorites.

Rob was tall, dark, and handsome. Approaching thirty. Exceptional physical shape. Mentally well-formed to be a killer, though he rarely needed to. Just enough of a sociopath to perform the work without becoming addicted to it, like some of them did.

Almost frighteningly perfect.

"I received a package this morning," Miguel began, switching his gaze back and forth between the two men seated across the vast desk from him. One hand possessively rested on the documents themselves. "Other intelligence agencies have no doubt received the same, or will in the near future. Somewhere, a timer has started and we need to do something. Rob, you start reading this now and hand pages to Ben as you complete them."

Both men had as close to eidetic memories as you got in this industry, sometimes able to actually pull up the image of a page years later and repeat it to you word for word. There weren't many pages here. Printed double space, with a good font and kerning, it only ran to thirty pages, plus a cover letter that had left Miguel cold as death when he read it.

As the men began digesting it, Miguel keyed the intercom, the smell of Rob's coffee sitting half-forgotten on Miguel's desk triggering his mind.

"Robin, could you have the kitchen send up a carafe of coffee?" he said when his right hand answered.

"On the way," Robin replied.

Miguel tried not to fidget as he waited. Mostly unsuccessfully. Coffee arrived and he refilled his mug from it.

Handsome finished and handed the last page to Ben with a grimace.

"Is she on the level?" Rob asked.

"As far as we know," Miguel replied. "I had the Records Department pull up anything we knew about the woman."

Miguel pulled another file from the stack and handed it to the man.

"Carlota Rojas," he informed them as Ben finished the last page. "Probable field name *Hummingbird*. What we know of her suggests a *Salonnian* agent who should be in her early fifties now. Reports hint that she was badly injured in the field four years ago, with a year of hospitalization and rehab after that. Apparently, at least according to what she purports to be Chapter One of a new tell-all memoir detailing her career and crimes, they forced her into what she feels is an unacceptable early retirement."

"And you think she'll really write the whole book and publish it everywhere?" Rob asked.

"If that's not a shot across however many bows, I'm not sure what is," Miguel replied.

"*Salonnia* will kill her when they catch her," Rob noted. "*Fribourg*, too. Hell, the Imperials might not even be polite about it when they find the woman. Lot of collateral damage might be acceptable, if she really knows that much about their operations and is willing to spill publicly. Double or triple that if she intends to have this published everywhere as about as lurid a memoir as you can manage."

Miguel nodded.

"What I need you two to tell me, literally off the cuff here, is if you think it might be worth jumping in with all the other hounds and trying to track her down," Miguel said. "It is the longest of longshots, but we have to play those occasionally."

Miguel leaned back and watched the two men cogitate. They knew hardly more than he did, other than the markings indicating that it had come from a trusted source. He kept folks on the payroll who worked for major publishers for exactly this reason. Money well invested, because more than once they had sent along a note.

Never had something this explosive come up, though.

"Are we trying to rescue her, or simply cause *Fribourg* and *Salonnia* an immense load of grief while they're trying to find her so they can shut her down?" Rob asked cogently. "Blow their budgets and maybe snag a few of their folks when nobody is looking because we want to be assholes?"

Miguel had spent an hour considering the exact same question. Other agents could cause havoc. Few would look beyond that for the chance to out or capture *Fribourg* agents for whatever information they might have or trade value.

"*Salonnia* will spare no expense trying to track down one

of their own gone rogue," Ben spoke up. "*Fribourg* as well, with, as Rob noted, a willingness to play extremely rough as they go. She sounds as though she knows more about *Fribourg* than *Aquitaine*, at least from the first set of accusations here."

"Will the Republic bite?" Rob chimed in. "We're their allies, however junior partners we are in the affair. What will they do?"

"I don't care," Miguel said. "If they got her, I doubt we'd learn any more than if the *Fribourg Empire* took her into custody. Possibly less. Rob, going back to your original question, if we could rescue her, I would consider that a coup for all the ages. Just being able to assemble better dossiers on agents from *Salonnia*, *Fribourg*, and even *Aquitaine* would be an exceptional win for us, because that gives us better visibility into what all our neighbors are up to. *Corynthe* might even send someone, but I doubt that the pirates care that much."

"Well, just sitting off to one side with a sniper rifle and a camera would be easy enough," Rob said. "Any of your agents could handle something so prosaic. I assume you want more from this operation?"

Miguel nodded.

"Find her, if possible," Miguel said. "Bring her in if you can. Turn her. Something. There is a wealth of information in her head beyond what she's threatened to spill to everyone with this book. What more could we learn.?Failing that, capturing enemy agents or just burning them covers the price of your admission, Rob."

"What are the operational limits involved?" Rob asked.

Yet another reason Rob was among the very best. He didn't suffer any sort of executive paralysis. Never got bogged down in theoretical questions. Simply found the edges of the sandbox itself and went to work.

"You'll be operating at extreme distances, Rob," Miguel said. "Communication will be impossible, because you can't know any of our normal operatives in place, lest they become unmasked in the soirée about to unfold."

The agent nodded. Assassin was a mindset as much as it was a job title. Frequently, they were alone at the sharpest edge of the spear. Rob excelled there, too.

"At the same time, I don't think I can put any meaningful limits on a field of battle almost entirely covered over in the fog of war, so you'll be working with as close to a blank check as I've ever signed, Handsome," Miguel continued, watching both men flinch in surprise.

Ben knew better than Rob what that meant, because any mistakes the field agent made would come up in hearings with Miguel's bosses, including the Privy Council and a few functionally invisible organizations within *Lincolnshire's* government.

"Going to have to travel fast and light," he mused, eyes locked on a point over Miguel's right shoulder. "Normally, I'd say alone, but if I can't tap resources when I get wherever, then I need to carry them along with me."

He paused and made eye contact, asking the obvious question.

"Are Mac and Alicia available for a fire drill?" Rob asked.

"They are," Miguel replied, nodding. That had been the first thing he'd checked on, after sending a note to have Rob come in today for a previously unscheduled meeting on what should have been his day off.

Not that the Service kept banker's hours, because his agents were constantly training, studying, qualifying, something. They still needed breaks to keep whatever sanity they had held onto for however long.

"How about an armorer?" Ben asked next, causing Rob to look that way.

"Nigel's on tour with Longbow and his band, last I checked," Rob said.

"Indeed," Miguel agreed. "Currently playing in one of the nearer sectors of *Aquitaine*, so we could get a message to them in a week or so, but nothing sooner."

"Too long," Ben said. "He needs to fly tonight if we're serious. Get ahead of the bow wave of the information if possible."

Bow wave. A measure of how quickly data could be carried between two points, as shown on a standard deviation curve. If you could move fast enough to be on the leading flat space, you could do things before folks were prepared for you to know anything about a project. Ben was right about the need to move immediately.

"I've put *Widowmaker* on standby, just in case," Miguel said. "Same yacht you took last time, to *Shravishtha Prime*. There have been a few upgrades added since then, based on your after-action reports. Awkward for four crew, but doable. Or we could find something larger, though not as fast."

"Speed kills," Rob said, sounding exactly like Jorge Royo when that man said it. "Crowded on a ship for a week isn't a problem. But I don't want to have to break someone in on the fly. Can you load me up with as much gear as you might send on a normal mission? I'll dig into my stuff and add some things. Make sure you ask Mac and Alicia what they'd bring, given a blank page. I'll need a copy of *Hummingbird's* folder, both paper and electronic, plus a few others. Whoever are the key players for *Fribourg* and *Aquitaine* operating in that sector of *Salonnian* space, plus the ones that know Rojas herself."

"You think they'll send her friends to kill her?" Ben asked.

"I think that they'll send people who know her, the better to get into her head," Rob countered. Miguel shared the assessment. "That woman doesn't seem to have friends, at least from what she's writing here. Or she's intent on burning them all and doesn't consider them friends anymore. The other side will need folks who might know how she thinks. Those will be the ones closest to her, so we can estimate who that might be. Nothing more."

"You are priority alpha, Rob," Miguel said. "Until you clear the atmosphere, you have a blank check for personnel, equipment, or intelligence, so you need to tell us what that is. I'll round up Mac and Alicia. Do you want to brief them?"

"No, you handle that," Rob said. "Tell them to pack for a sudden mission, given the planet in question, and meet me on the ship for details. I need to wander down to the canteen and figure out what I'll need to carry with me, and what I can find when I get there."

The man rose and moved to the door.

"Anything else right now?"

"Not at the moment," Miguel said. "Cover identity papers and legends will be worked up as you have lunch. Everything else will be in motion."

Rob nodded and left. Ben had remained seated.

"Think he can do it?" Ben asked.

"I don't think anybody else can, Ben," Miguel answered.

Not the same thing, but at least it was honest.

Was the galaxy really ready for someone to air all the dirty laundry they might know?

That was the real question.

What lengths would *Fribourg* or *Salonnia* go to, in order to silence the woman, before anybody else could pick her brain?

3

ESMERALDA MACTAVISH. GENERALLY KNOWN AROUND the building as Mac. Today, she was aboard the yacht *Widowmaker*. Reading in the kitchen.

Formerly, Head of the Service's Data Analysis Inspectorate, before a taste of field operations had convinced her that she liked it more than the dry numbers of advanced, applied mathematics. She'd worked directly with Rob twice, as well as training with him in a variety of tasks.

Miguel kept her on the active agent roster to use as an older woman who could provide a solid cover for Handsome, as if he was a clueless boy-toy she'd brought along. There weren't many older men still working, once you got beyond Jorge Royo. But the game worked exceptionally well, since she was still almost the same size she'd been as a model thirty years ago. Gray hair in stripes natually these days, except that she'd been instructed to turn it all dark blond now for a mission that had come out of the blue.

Completely out of the blue, even, as she'd been scheduled to teach an advanced class in analytics programming to some of the newer staff later in the week. Alicia could have taught it as well, but was also packed and ready to move.

Fire drill, as they said on the operations side of the building. Miguel says jump and everybody asked how high on the way up.

She looked up as the main hatch opened and Handsome Rob stepped in. They'd been lovers professionally, under cover of a legend on a mission, but never spoke of it when they were home. Might be time again, but she wasn't sure.

All Miguel had said when pulling her in was to pack and be ready to leave the planet in eight hours.

And here she was.

"Alicia is bunking in the pilot's cabin," Mac said as he dropped an overnight bag and an extremely heavy duffel bag next to the table where she sat. "At least for now."

That gave him the option to take the pilot space for himself and put the two women together if he wanted. Or needed. He was nice to snuggle with, but this was a blank piece of paper and it felt like Rob was making everything up as he went.

Something had gone very desperately wrong.

Again.

"Good enough," he said, nodding and kneeling.

She watched him pull a big folder out of the overnight bag and hand it to her.

"I'm going to do preflight and then take off while you read this," he said. "Have Alicia do the same."

Then he was gone forward.

Mac listened to the ship make new noises as Rob did all his piloting things, but that was background noise.

She read.

Carlota Rojas. *Salonnian* spy probably once named *Hummingbird*. Angry at her fate and striking back, from the tone of the cover letter and Chapter One of the new book she was mailing to various places. Willing to share everything she'd learned in thirty years of espionage, just to get even.

"Stand by for lift off," Rob said over the intercom, followed by the ship shivering as he got everything in motion.

Rob was as good a pilot as he was lover, so she wouldn't even have spilled any of the coffee she had, even had it not been in a sippy cup for zero gravity. Alicia emerged and Mac handed her pages to read.

Eventually, she finished the documents. Wasn't all that much, but it was about as damning as it got, especially if Rojas was serious about naming names behind various assassinations and acts of what might not have been random terrorism.

Fribourg was an empire and wouldn't care all that much if the truth came out, but *Aquitaine* would still like to use that to drive wedges into the general population over there. And it wasn't like anybody had clean hands.

"Shit," Alicia muttered when she finished.

Mac studied the woman. One of the smartest folks in the building, a physics major with a secondary specialization in cryptographic mathematics. Once upon a time, she had been short, dumpy, and just at the edge of failing various regular physical fitness qualifications that the Service maintained. The data nerds spent most of their time staring at screens in dark rooms, rather than running obstacle courses like Rob.

Alicia Sepeda had found that she liked the field work she'd done last year with Handsome. She was by no means slinky, to say nothing of as slender as Mac, but Alicia had set up a treadmill at her desk and routinely walked a minimum of twenty thousand steps in the course of a single workday.

She liked to say she had good Polish peasant genes, but that just meant thighs and a bottom, both as big and strong as most men.

"Shit," Alicia repeated. "Is this woman insane?"

"Angry," Mac replied. "When Rob's done up front, I'll share some of my thoughts."

Alicia nodded and walked carefully downhill to the coffee maker and got herself another mug. Rob had brought the local grav-plates on line, but left them at low power until he was higher out of the atmosphere. The room sloped weirdly, but Rob was excellent at what he did, and everything balanced nicely.

Time passed, but not that much. Rob must have been in a hurry if they were already high enough that he could engage the autopilot to come back to talk to them.

"Let's talk on the bridge," Mac suggested as he appeared.

He nodded, retreating, and she followed, Alicia in her wake.

The bow was wide, spanning the entire four-meter width of the interior as it narrowed down towards the prow. Only two piloting stations, but several jumpseats around the sides and back. She directed Alicia into one where everyone could see each other, even as she took the seat next to Rob.

"Thoughts on first pass?" he asked.

"She's my age, Rob," Mac replied.

"That was one of the reasons I wanted you," he nodded. "I'm younger and male. I presume there will be things wrapped up in her age and gender that I'll miss. I presume that everyone else is likely to make similar mistakes unless they send the right kind of woman along."

She liked the way he danced elegantly around the fact that she was old enough to be his mother. The *right* kind of woman?

Mac paused and considered what that would be, were she in this woman's shoes, relative stranger or not.

"She's smart," Mac said. "And not just smart, but brilliant in a cagey kind of way. Maybe not pure intellectual firepower like Alicia and me, but she reads like a chameleon who can vanish into any group of people so fast that you miss her walking through the door."

"I got that same impression," Rob nodded, mostly watching her and Alicia but both hands still on the control yoke as the darkness out the front windows got wider and deeper.

"So I'm going to put myself into her shoes and just let things come out of my mouth, okay?" Mac continued.

"Hold on," Alicia said, rising and pressing a button on the console. "Okay, recording you now."

"Good idea," Rob noted. "Talk."

"So I'm fifty, and one of the best agents they have," Mac surmised. "Something goes wrong on some mission, but I don't think it's my fault. Still, I end up in the hospital for a while, then in a home, rebuilding myself physically."

"Check you so far," Rob said.

"Then I think I'm ready to go back out into the field, but the men in charge decide to put me out to pasture instead," Mac continued, unable to help the growl in her voice from growing more pronounced.

Miguel had let her stay with field agent training, even though she was supposedly far too old for it. She was keeping up physically with men fresh out of spy school. She wasn't Rob's match, but not that many men or women in the building were. However, if Miguel retired or was replaced, odds were good that she'd be pulled back into the old Data Analysis Inspectorate, even though they had a new boss now to replace her.

Or forcibly retired like Carlota.

"Worse," Mac said as a light bulb came on in her head. "I'm put on a desk somewhere. Maybe handling routine decryption or communications traffic, because I'm expert in the field lingo. Or they put me down in Records and tell me they are doing me a favor until I can collect a full pension, rather than a medical disability version where I'd have to be inspected like a side of meat every few years."

Rob glanced over at the vitriol dripping into her voice, but Mac ignored him. Turned to Alicia instead and let their womanliness bond. *Salonnia* was run by men, just like *Fribourg*. At least *Lincolnshire* and *Aquitaine* allowed women to advance, but the men across the border ran things.

Men.

"I'm still too young to just sit behind a desk and molder until I hit some magic age," Mac growled at Alicia.

"And I'm angry at everyone responsible," the other woman growled back, getting into the abject chauvinism of it. "I need to get even, but they'll come after me hard when I do. Everything I've ever said or done will be reviewed closely when I go rogue."

"Ergo," Mac nodded. "I need to access my personnel file, down in Records. Swap things out or simply wipe it clean before I start this. Before I retire, and nobody realized it until I was out of the building, running as hard as I could to build up a head start."

"Did I start writing while I was still employed, or does that come later?" Alicia asked.

"Later," Mac decided. "I won't commit treason while on active duty, but once I'm retired, a free agent, I'm going to go out in a blaze of glory so hot that everyone else goes with me. You've seen just what she mentioned in Chapter One, detailing all the cases and things coming in future installments."

"Why not just publish it?" Rob asked. "Why not drop the entire manuscript on a publishing house and let them get it delivered to bookstores and onto various networks before anybody can stop you?"

"Because I have to prove that I'm smarter than them,

Rob," Mac snapped. "That I still had what it took to be a field agent. That they fucked up by putting me at a desk. The longer I can run, the more I prove that I was better than them."

"And what's your endgame?" Rob asked.

Mac paused, crestfallen. She turned to Alicia and caught the moment of confusion on that woman's face as well.

"I'm not sure I ever thought about it," Mac said. "I got so wrapped up in my own self that it became a game."

"Indeed," Rob nodded. "However, now pretend that I'm various intelligence agencies all over the damned galaxy. I'm coming for you. Some of us want to shut you down or kill you entirely for what you're going to do. Others want to take you alive so they can suck you dry like a leech and discover everything that might be contained in that dangerously smart, beautiful head of yours. Do you have an out at the end, or do I hunt you until you're dead or taken?"

Mac collapsed back against her seat as she saw where Rob's intuition had taken him. It was laid out perfectly, seen from the side, but she'd been running down in the middle of it, reveling in the ability to hit back at everyone that had hurt her.

Most women in societies run by men knew that feeling. That power. That freedom.

Those same men would see her challenge their power, and move to crush it. And they had more resources. More people. More money.

More rage, however slow it might be to build.

It would be implacable.

"I think I end up dead," Mac said quietly.

Rob nodded.

Silence took them all.

There had to be a way to survive all this.

Didn't there?

4

CARLOTA KNEW SHE WAS TAKING A HORRIBLE CHANCE doing this, but the game had finally matured, and she wanted to run a few noses into things. Not enough to get caught, but sufficient to remind the men in the fancy suits behind heavy desks that they should have listened to her.

Gods, that metaphorical pat on the head by the Administrator of the Bureau on that last day.

Walking across the casino floor, she remembered every bit of it with a rage that almost felt like she should catch fire.

Grendel Montague—what a name—sitting behind his desk scowling at her.

"Rojas, I've called you in here because I'm getting reports that you're unhappy, down in Recordkeeping," he'd said to her.

Even today, she could still smell that tacky aftershave his stupid wife had bought for him for some holiday. The man wore it everywhere, reminding her of cheap tarts sitting in windows with red lights on, passing the time and catcalling sailors walking by.

And his suit had been let out just about as far as it could, and that still hadn't been enough. Should have tossed it and bought a new wardrobe. The man had the money. Either that or he should have started enforcing those same standards on himself that everyone else had to meet at least semi-annually.

But she'd sat, primly, hands clasped on her knee. Carlota had even happened to be wearing a long dress that day, like some soap opera housewife who had wandered into the wrong scene by accident during live filming, leaving everyone to improvise.

She was an expert at improv. One had to be when people around you had pistols aimed in your general direction.

"Has there been any complaints about my work, sir?" she'd asked him, dark brown eyes aimed like deadly weapons at the man.

Physically, Carlota was blessed, at least in certain ways. Slightly better than average looks. Nothing that would stop traffic. Nothing *memorable*. Brown hair nearly white now if she let the roots go. Dark eyes. Dark brown skin that almost made her look Aquitainian compared to others.

Invisible. Bad when trying to work in sales. Perfect in espionage.

"Your work has been spotless, Rojas," Montague groused at her, leaned back and playing with a pen like a miniature baton. "Frankly, it's your attitude."

"Sir?"

"Bureau psychologists don't think you should be in the field, Rojas," he said, leaning forward to put a hand down firmly. Like squishing her to the desk in his mind.

"And I believe you are all wrong, Administrator," Carlota replied with a petite smile and the slightest twist of her head.

Montague shuddered under her assault, possibly without even realizing what or why.

She was good at that. Getting inside a man's mind and planting suggestions.

Montague was just too bullheaded to allow her any leverage.

It didn't help that he had spent most of this meeting staring at her tits instead of her eyes.

I have a face, you asshole.

But he hadn't listened.

"Well, my decision is final, Rojas," he'd growled finally. "You need to get with the boat, or get off it."

She'd considered her options. They'd offered her a medical pension. Nothing great, but she had funds hidden in various banks and other places.

"That's it?" she'd asked.

"That's it, Rojas."

"In that case, my resignation will be on your desk this afternoon, Administrator," she'd said.

And walked out.

And done some things that they wouldn't catch until later.

And resigned.

Had an entire year passed?

Carlota had been watching the casino floor as she moved through the crowd like a tide ebbing and flowing around her. Tonight, she'd dressed in a long, silk sheath in light green that was off one shoulder, sliced nearly to the other thigh, and seemed to be hung slightly askew. Across her body instead of along it.

Her tan was perfect.

As with Montague, many of the men never made it far enough up to see she had a face, studying the tantalizing bits she was displaying. Her bra pushed her breasts up and fuller than normal, just to accentuate things. Her long legs ended in stiletto heels nearly twelve centimeters long, making her the equal of most men and taller than many.

She approached a sour-faced man behind a lectern,

guarding a closed door near a corner of the game floor. He wore a suit off the rack that hadn't been tailored, so she marked him as an employee of the casino.

"Tamblin Bernard," she said a little breathlessly as she got close enough to speak over the quiet roar of machines and conversations behind her. She even leaned forward a little to draw his eyes down. Worked like a charm. "I'm on your list."

"Do you have your invitation?" he asked in a grumpy, bored tone, not even enthusiastic enough to ogle her.

Carlota wasn't sure if she should be insulted or not. Certainly, the man wouldn't remember much of her later, when asked by folks no doubt busy chasing her.

Carlota sighed in a way that literally heaved her bosom at the man. Rolled her eyes just a little to get into the character of a put-upon princess.

Then she got mean.

Carlota turned slightly, presenting the right leg, the one that was open to nearly her hip so the man could see it. She even pulled the front back like a curtain displaying her lovely leg.

And the bridal garter she wore around her perfectly-smooth thigh.

That got his eyes bulging a little. And a few pedestrians with the amazing luck to be walking nearby at the right moment.

Carlota removed the invitation card from the garter and looked at it for a moment. No larger than a standard business card, printed on exceptionally heavy stock and hand-printed in the name of the person she was playing tonight as she'd wandered onto somebody else's set.

The garter on her left thigh had a small knife tucked in on the inside, out of sight, razor sharp on both edges and perfectly balanced for throwing, if necessary.

It had been years since she'd needed it as anything but a conversation piece in a seduction.

As Tamblin Bernard, she handed the card to the man, not bothering to close up the possible view of heaven that held his attention.

Leg man. Good to know.

Men were visual creatures. Useful intelligence to learn what this one's triggers were.

He made a point of checking the card against a clipboard that he'd had hidden inside the lectern. Smiled at her. Handed it back without losing the smile.

Carlota rewarded him by replacing it where it had been.

Letting him see something he'd never get a chance to touch, as it were.

There must be a buzzer somewhere that she'd missed, because the door behind the man opened now and a tiny woman in a painful-looking black and red corset opened it and bowed to her.

"This way, madame," she said.

Carlota followed her through the door, into the back rooms where the big pots occurred.

The game had gotten a little tame. A little stale.

Carlota needed to stir things up again.

5

CARLOTA FOLLOWED THE WOMAN INTO A LARGE ROOM with a dozen doors leading to smaller rooms. Two were open currently, revealing private card rooms with games adjourned or not yet started. The place ran around the clock, but even the most diehard players eventually succumbed to exhaustion.

At least one presumed. Chemicals and stubbornness could push that deadline off a considerable distance, but sooner or later you started making mistakes.

Scoring goals in your own net.

In her previous line of work—and her current one—such things would quickly prove deadly.

Carlota approached everything with studious deliberation. Including poker.

It was an ancient sport, both of kings and peasants. Only the scale of the stakes really differed. People sitting around a table with cards in front of them and money piled in ever-changing sizes as luck, intuition, and intestinal fortitude held sway.

The gender ratio in here was normal for this sort of

situation. Five men for every woman. At least among the players. The reverse held for the staff, with most of the women chosen for bustiness that could be crammed into something uncomfortably tight around the middle, creating a figure visually top and bottom heavy.

She loathed corsets. And the men who decided women needed to wear them to be sexy.

Salonnia had many things that were beyond her power to fix, but gods in hell below, there were days she wanted to try. Bring down far more than just the Bureau. Preferably with fire.

Let the ashes cool and hope something better would arise from the ruins.

It might be difficult to do worse.

Still, these places existed. And money changed hands.

She had stashed away a tremendous number of credits over the years. Operational funds never accounted for at the end of an operation. Free cash confiscated when raiding an enemy agent, or taking one into custody. Or catching someone just as he thought he might defect, with an entire suitcase of various bills from various places.

That suitcase had been marked destroyed in the firefight.

Technically not true. Carlota had destroyed it much later, after emptying it into a different valise.

She didn't need money right now.

The game in her head required her to travel. To make a splash in various places. While always looking over her shoulder for agents who might finally catch up with her.

Chapters Two and Three were posted, the first slow burn leading up to the really fun disclosures in Chapter Twelve. That was the one that she'd sworn an oath to never disclose on pain of death. The rest were just good for centuries in prison.

Someone would be coming for her. Soon. If they weren't

already on their way. But the galaxy was a big place. Easy enough to vanish if she really wanted. There were false papers and complete identities stashed on a number of planets, along with funds she could draw on.

That broke the rules of the game she had invented, though.

The Bureau had to have a chance to stop her. Had to have everything waved under their nose like a red flag. That would bring *Fribourg* assassins and *Aquitaine* spies sniffing, with everyone stumbling over each other and causing more chaos.

Three men in tailored tuxedos checked her up one side and down the other as she approached, as if she might be in one of the pots they won later and could claim her as a prize.

One of them wasn't half-bad looking. The second was homely. The third reminded her of stories she'd heard as a child of bog trolls clattering at the window sill at night, trying to get in and steal unruly children.

"Here to play?" the middle man asked.

"Looking for a challenge," she fired back, seeing if he might rise to strike the bait.

Looks weren't everything. Even with bog trolls.

"Hoping for some game," the semi-handsome one offered. "Stretch things out and see what there was to see."

Her thigh was jutted out enoug—uncovered enough—to distract. His eyes caressed her whole body as he spoke.

Poker was a game of focus. Of insight into complete strangers across a green felt table, with pots frequently equal to an office drone's monthly salary. And occasionally his annual one.

Bog troll grunted and ignored her.

The floor manager approached, his suit better tailored than the man outside.

"Welcome, guests," he gushed quietly as he took them all

in. "Is four sufficient or would you like to wait a bit to see who else might join?"

Carlota turned to one side and studied the room. A dozen other folks sat at tables or in chairs around the outside, relaxing, smoking, or just drinking. Perhaps they'd cashed out, or gone broke.

Or just needed time to decompress.

Carlota could not relax. She would be dead before she knew what hit her if she did.

Two fat merchants in off-the-rack suits came through the outer door as she watchec. The three men around her stirred like wolves smelling sheep. Studying the men, she had to agree. They looked like small-time players that thought they had fast-talked someone into an invite to the private rooms, rather than walking banks accounts needing to be emptied before they were sent home.

She made eye contact with the barely younger of the two, maybe only forty and slightly less squishy.

Slightly.

Carlota extended her smile in his direction and drew the man to them like magic, pulling his companion along with him like a tide going out. The floor manager turned sideways and watched with a knowing smile.

"We were just about to start a game," Carlota offered to the men with the same breathlessness that seemed to work on most of them. "Were you here to play?"

The eyes on the older of the two nearly bugged out as he stared at her outfit. She wondered if they were from some quaint, agricultural world that didn't have anything remotely like this casino.

Along with whatever other evils you could get into in a place without windows looking in or clocks nagging you.

"Gosh, that'd be swell," the younger man said earnestly.

Something was off in his accent, but she couldn't

immediately place it. It didn't fit the suit somehow, and she'd spent three decades mentally peeling away façades to find the spies underneath.

Briefly, Carlota wondered if some bureau stringer had thought to look in a high-stakes poker suite and gotten lucky to see someone that might be his quarry.

Not that she looked at all like the woman she'd been a year ago.

Or the stranger she'd assembled to replace her personnel file in those few hours between realizing that she was done and turning in her badge for the last time.

Paper had actually worked in her favor, there at the end. Electronic files could be accessed remotely and tampered with, sometimes without anyone realizing it, or at least not until it was too late to do anything about it. So everything was paper and long-term storage on film that would last for centuries.

Until someone swapped a roll when checking it in. And then accidentally put in a blank cartridge somewhere else, after thirty-seven such mistakes had been returned to salt-mine storage off sight.

The only records they had of her now were mental. People who had known her personally, or at least on sight.

Carlota figured that it would give all the other players an edge if *Salonnia* started off so badly handicapped. *Fribourg* might have images of her from as recent as twelve or fifteen years ago, depending. They might be able to age them up and get close.

At least until the Bureau told them that part of putting her back together after the...*incident*...had involved rebuilding her face. Subtle, to be sure, but her jawline was different. Her cheekbones had been enhanced just a little in an effort to balance out the broken bones for healing. The chin was softer.

And she'd let her hair go completely gray while recovering and as she spent time punching a stupid clock at a worthless desk.

Tonight, she presented as a thirty-eight-year-old social widow who had watched her foolish husband run off with a waitress, before cleaning him out in the divorce and starting to play the field.

In more ways than one.

It was a role she had played a few times when she'd been younger, when an overt honeypot had been more effective. The Vamp Years, as she recalled them mentally; the idiots in charge ordered her to present as a bubbly teenager too dumb to be a threat to big, bad, enemy agents.

At least until she got them asleep afterwards and could either kill them or inject a quick soporific that kept them entirely docile until pickup teams came to retrieve them.

Too many men led entirely astray by the divining rod between their legs.

Still, the two men didn't strike her as spies. Not directly. Observers, maybe.

Bog troll had already entered the game room, so she gestured her two new marks in and let the two other men in tuxedos have a view of her bottom as they followed her.

The room was large but cozy, done in muted greens and blues that left it feeling larger than it was, while still keeping everything calm and pleasant. Octagonal table, limiting play nicely to eight, though she supposed that there might be larger tables in some of the other rooms. Comfortable chairs.

An uncomfortable waitress in a leather sausage casing accompanied them in and got drink orders. The floor manager delivered two decks of brand new cards, still in the wrapping.

The players took the stage.

Bog troll had ended up in the farthest corner from the

door, with the two other tuxedos flanking him on either side. Carlota had gone right instead of left, putting her flash of thigh side next to the prettiest of the three sharks, rather than the two salesmen.

They were about to be bled dry. She saw no reason to pile on by distracting them any more than she needed to.

Plus, this way she could use that view on the one shark who held himself like an expert player.

She might need him thinking about getting her naked instead of calculating odds and counting cards.

The ancient game had been focused on odd numbers, using four suits of thirteen cards each. In the old times, you got two cards dealt, one up and one hidden, then bet. After that, a third card. Then a fourth. Then a fifth.

There was a variant with seven cards dealt, but you ended up burning most of the deck each hand when you had eight players. Six here was less complicated.

Still, the bog troll spoke.

"Six hand stud?" he asked, in a voice remarkably clear and crisp on such an ugly man.

Truly, a face for radio.

Carlota had played almost every variant of stud poker in the galaxy. Six was a rarer one. It caused the math to be far more obscure than five or seven.

She wondered if that was a comment on the other two wolves in the room with him, as the man hadn't yet identified her as a serious player.

He would learn soon enough.

Everyone assented and began to pull cash to buy chips.

She wondered how interesting things would get.

6

————

CARLOTA STUDIED THE REMAINING PLAYERS.

On one hand, three hours had passed relatively quickly. Even pleasantly.

On the other, the bog troll was a serious player on a whole other level from the two men in tuxedos who had been standing around when she first arrived. The middle of those three was already bust and gone, along with the older of the two salesmen.

That left her, the younger salesman, the prettier male, and the bog troll with the lovely radio voice.

The remaining tux liked to be called Donel, but he wasn't going to be around long enough to matter. And flop sweat was among the most unsexy things Carlota knew.

But that was why you played games like this. To see who the serious players were, and who were mere poseurs to be discounted fairly quickly.

The younger salesman was named William. Not Bill, like his friend might have done. William. Spoken with seriousness the one and only time he'd needed to correct anyone.

Carlota had split her attention between William and the bog troll, who was really named Armand. She could sit and listen to Armand read a comm directory.

She and William had come out a little ahead over the last few hours, until she was up about eighty-five thousand cedis right now. Not what she'd hoped for tonight, but she also hadn't been expecting someone like Armand at the table.

Ringer.

Only four of them left, with Donel obviously needing to win the next hand to remain. The other two were already outside the room. William dealt.

Carlota studied her two cards, both Empresses in gold and blue. A powerful leading hand.

She raised Donel's two hundred to five hundred and everyone called. Just marking her scent on this one, so far. She'd bluffed a few hands tonight with nothing better, at times when some of the other players had been willing to fold instead of paying for knowledge.

Armand had a red Jester showing.

The next round delivered her a Seven of Stones. Worthless, but nobody else was feeling bold enough to challenge. Or to push Donel entirely out by raising more than he might have on his person or available to call on sudden credit.

Armand had added a red Emperor to it, suggesting that he was going for a straight or possibly a royal flush, depending on colors. Betting got a little stronger, but nobody folded.

William had a pair of sevens showing and started betting and raising as if he had the third one down. Carlota called but didn't push things, as she'd gotten the black Empress, giving her three of a kind and a mathematical edge, depending on Armand.

Donel was down to a few hundred cedis at this point. He grinned when the bet came around and folded.

"I'm just not feeling it tonight," he said with a shrug, picking up his last few chips and tossing them into the pot so he could walk away without taking anything.

It didn't make that much of a difference, but it caused the room to pause for a long moment as he exited, trying to put on a brave face for her that Carlota didn't find all that appetizing after watching him at his most emotional.

Armand was actually a more interesting person, from the tidbits he'd let drop.

Carlota's only worry at this point was that William really was a stringer for somebody's espionage agency and had recognized her. His partner had been the first to exit broke, but that also gave the man the perfect excuse to slip out and call for backup.

Not many people would be dumb enough to try to take her in here. Casino security would see them as potential armed robbers and drop a planetary moon's worth of trouble on them immediately, before trying to sort things out later.

They took a dim view of threats to their customers.

However, they might try to follow her later. As if Carlota had just innocently decided to come to this casino and spend several hours in a single public place, playing.

Fools.

Armand had sneered at Donel's back as he left. Carlota turned back just fast enough to catch it. They shared a smile and he nodded like a schoolboy caught sneaking out at night.

The next round of cards caused William to bet heavily, raising every time it came to him. Armand was pushing the man in ways he hadn't before, as if he'd developed a sudden antipathy to the salesman.

Or wanted to get rid of everyone else so he could have a clear chance to seduce the woman.

Bog troll, certainly. But a mannered one. And smart. With a baritone voice that just soothed her nerves to listen to. She might not say yes, but she wouldn't immediately say no either.

Life was to be lived. That had been what had driven her to take such insane risks in the first place. Montague expected her to sit passively at a desk filing paperwork and answering questions for people who had never held a gun, let alone used it on someone.

Until she turned sixty or something, changing into a withered husk of a woman forgotten in the basement because those men upstairs couldn't imagine that any woman was their equal in competence, to say nothing of their better.

And most of them thought that a woman had already lost her bloom by thirty. Morons.

She'd just been getting started.

Finally, everyone settled in, but the pot was over one hundred thousand cedis now. And there were still two cards left.

She'd be more worried if Armand was dealing, but William had the cards and hadn't struck her as the kind of sharp who could deal off the bottom as needed.

Could he?

Was that the secret? Two men, one an expert player who could force things and string them out all night, while the other called for the cavalry?

Salonnia wouldn't know her for gambling. Not unless they went back and interviewed a few folks who had retired out of the building a decade or more ago. And her personnel file had evaporated, if you wanted to look something up.

That left memories.

Or maybe he was an outsider? *Fribourg*? *Aquitaine*? Someplace even more exotic?

They might have files on her. Not great, but a definite

head start on the locals. She'd done that on purpose, to make the game more equitable.

And to show everybody in the galaxy that she was still a top-notch agent and player.

William dealt Armand the red ten, suggesting a royal flush was coming. Carlota got a blue six. William got a gold four. Betting and raising got ugly again, as if William thought he could push the other two out of the game. She matched him. Armand did as well.

The pot was approaching two hundred thousand cedis. A lot of money for an evening, let alone a single hand of poker.

She listened to William speak as he got excited. There was a verbal tic there. A falseness in his tones that she could detect. They were speaking in Arabic tonight, but he had a strange accent, as if English might be his native tongue.

Definitely not *Salonnian*, then. Possibly *Aquitaine*, but they tended towards Bulgarian as the main tongue, though many folks were bi- and tri-lingual, depending on where someone might live.

English more strongly suggested the *Fribourg Empire* had gotten here finally. They had the farthest distance to travel, assuming they hadn't activated local assets.

Or did they wish to keep those spies hidden yet, as they would need to work closely with *Salonnian* authorities and agents?

One didn't want to give away everything. That would be like walking into the room naked. Useful once, but then you didn't have any surprises left to spring on someone later.

Last card, dealt face down like the first one. One less round that a seven-card version, with that much thinner odds to make your best five cards from. But down, unlike five-card.

Secret.

Open for interpretation. For bluffing.

For lying.

"Ten thousand cedis," William opened, even before Carlota had looked at her card.

Armand studied his hole card and smiled like he'd just drawn what he needed. With the Emperor, Jester, and Ten of Swords—all red—showing, he could be sitting on the Crown Prince and Empress he needed to take any pot.

"Raise forty thousand," Armand said in a friendly tone. He turned to Carlota. "Fifty to you."

She knew within a few hundred how many cedis were piled haphazardly in front of her, unlike the ordered piles of the two men.

She pulled her sixth card and slumped slightly. Not much. The sort of thing that might be interpreted as an unconscious twitch. As if there was anything like it at this table. William was an exceptional player, but she had math on her side. He was pushing, but she was dead certain that the man was bluffing.

Or buying time. There was always that.

Armand was a ringer. She'd like to sit in a gallery sometime, just to watch him put on a master class in poker for players who thought they were the shit. As he methodically cleaned every single one of them out.

The last Empress stared back at her, winking almost.

Carlota willed her entire body to perfect stillness . Not that of a statue, but not that of a woman who had just drawn the red Empress that Armand would have needed to complete his hand. Four Empresses. With what he had, the man couldn't be sitting on anything more than three of a kind.

William might have four sevens. She couldn't be sure without paying for the privilege, but she was certain now that Armand was bluffing. Hard, but he had all that excess cash in front of him that he could afford to.

Carlota mulled her options with a platinum chip in one hand.

"Fifty?" she confirmed, just to watch William fidget with unnecessary energy.

Had he meant to send Armand the red Empress and screwed up his count? It was possible. It was also possible that this was an honest deal.

She'd have to brace the man and then probably read his personnel file to be sure, assuming a *Fribourg* agent in the field.

"Sure, I'll call that," she offered with a shrug in her voice, counting and tossing in a number of five-thousand-cedi chips from the back and bottom of her pile.

There were still an awful lot of chips in front of her.

"Call and raise," William snapped, throwing more chips into the enormous pile growing between them. "Another fifty thousand."

That left him without a lot of chips left. Carlota had just fallen below breaking even for the evening, entertainment notwithstanding. Armand smiled like a shark and counted a strange number of chips.

"Fine," he said. "And I'll raise you fourteen thousand, six hundred, and ten cedis. That will leave you enough for dinner."

Carlota just barely managed to keep her jaw from falling open. That looked like a remarkably accurate assessment of what William had in front of him at this exact moment, minus maybe fifty for food later.

Armand smiled at her. It was a friendly smile, as opposed to the harshness he'd reserved for Donel and others earlier. He had to know he couldn't beat William. Why was he doing this?

She counted nearly sixty-five thousand cedis and slid them into the pot. Now, she was in bad shape, if she lost.

Carlota had come in here tonight to win enough money that she could live nicely for a couple of years without having to risk tapping into any banks or places where someone might have once remembered her having an account. All the better to vanish.

That, and she'd gotten a little bored sitting in hotel rooms. Earlier, she'd had the manuscript to keep her occupied, typing all those memories into a system and reviewing the lives she intended to destroy.

The careers she would burn because they'd taken hers away.

If I can't have it, neither can you.

William counted his chips, and had fifty-three cedis left, which just added another level of complexity and interestingness to Armand.

There was a long moment of silence, then Armand smiled and turned over his cards.

"Three tens," he said.

William bounced triumphantly in his chair.

"Full house!" he declared. "Sevens over threes."

Both men turned to her expectantly, almost forgotten in the macho testosterone of those last few hands. Armand even had the faintest grin on his face, while William's was shifting over into a sour scowl that felt more like the man he was at home.

"Four Empresses," she said, flipping over the other two.

William's face fell. Armand grinned like the kid that had gotten a perfect score on a surprise quiz.

She had somewhere close to half a million cedis piled up in front of her.

"I think that we're probably done now," Armand announced in that radio voice.

He rose and bowed to her, moving to the door and opening it to gesture the floor manager inside to assist.

Carlota would need a valise to carry just the chips, but the manager brought two young studs with canvas bags, who began shoveling things.

William rose in defeat, utter disbelief on his face.

It was as if no woman had ever beaten him at a card table in his life.

She rather enjoyed taking his virginity, if that was what it was.

The man staggered out past Armand, still standing next to the doorway.

The floor manager and his men departed.

Carlota was a bit dumbfounded herself, but she'd just extended the run of her own game against every intelligence agency in the galaxy for a long time.

Hopefully, she hadn't used up all her luck in the process. She was going to need it later, when the other players got desperate.

She made eye contact with Armand, the man she had thought of as a bog troll at first glance.

"May I be so bold as to invite you to dinner, madame?" he asked, bowing again.

She rose and tried to assemble the entire evening into a coherent narrative, but it eluded her.

"Someplace quiet," she said, a little uncertain.

Armand glanced back at the open door, and everyone that might lurking just out of sight.

"I know a place where they'll never find you," he beamed.

She found herself smiling back at the man.

7
_____

Rob had pushed the ship. Hard. Ben had mentioned earlier the need to outrun news, getting to the place that rumors suggested might be the current hiding place of *Hummingbird*.

He was just about ready to drop down to the planet, having completed most of his orbital checklist.

Widowmaker had been souped up some since last year. Mostly an extra generator for the JumpSails, wedged in aft in such a way that he really wouldn't want to have to pull maintenance on the life support systems anywhere that he didn't have a dedicated and specialized garage. Like the Service had.

According to the standard sailing directions, it should take you on the order of eight days run to get to *Borlait* from *Ramsey* in *Lincolnshire*, flying a normal, commercial ship. He had just dropped out of orbit in a little more than five. Assuming that Miguel had moved immediately when he first got the files on Carlota Rojas, there might be a week before anybody expected *Salonnia*'s oldest rival to make an appearance.

Lincolnshire and *Salonnia* had never been important players. Both were small nations on the outer fringes of major powers, *Aquitaine* and *Fribourg* respectively. And allies of those two as well. Deadly enemies across the border occasionally, but mostly just two kids bitching at each other in a sandbox.

But the local politics and culture clash went back centuries, with *Lincolnshire* being more culturally rural and *Salonnia* being best known for the criminal syndicates that ran everything and usually just owned the necessary politicians outright.

Everyone was at peace right now. More or less. Enough that he could list a fictitious departure from Giovanni in *Lincolnshire* and fake a lazy course to the playgrounds of *Borlait* and not raise many suspicions or complaints from the locals.

A year ago, he and Mac had gone to *Shravishtha Prime*. *Salonnia* was known for a string of resort-centered worlds along several of their borders, like pearls hanging in the darkness. All the better to liberate foreigners from their cash. As well as smuggle things in and out.

It wasn't like the laws of *Salonnia*, already looser than anywhere else, were ever enforced if you had the spare cash to bribe someone.

Borlait itself was almost a company town according to the notes he had devoured. Bennan was the capital, a huge urban center that mostly existed to provide a ready pool of employees for the many hotels, resorts, and everything else around it in rings. You landed at the starport, took a train to the center of town and then caught spokes out to where you were going.

From space, if you squinted, it was almost an eye, with the pupil as Bennan and the rest as a thinly populated white.

Rob had decided to avoid the expense and publicity of

hiring a private car to take them to their hotel. It wasn't that far from the station, and he had already expected a number of spies and agents to be running around.

Soon, they would be so thick that you might need a playbill with headshots attached to keep track of them. Which was exactly why he was here. If nothing else, there ought to be monumental opportunities to capture images of various spies who could then be researched and circulated later.

Plus, he had a trump card. Two of them, really. Mac quietly had, in many ways, all the issues that Rojas would, which would help him get inside the other woman's mind. Additionally, Alicia had been constantly overlooked and belittled by anyone outside of her own Inspectorate. The Numbers Nerds, as folks in Operations occasionally derided them. She had a quiet rage, hidden inside.

He knew better. Doubly so after sharing a mission with two such women in the past. These women were experts who just didn't break and enter with a gun in one hand like so many agents and vid shows seemed to think was how it worked.

It had taken Alicia so little time to hack the resort's security system before that she'd been afraid that it was a trap. Only later had she been professionally insulted.

Rob had had to explain to her how good those systems really were, and by extension how good she was at that sort of thing. At least he'd gotten through.

But he could tap that resentment that she'd known. Rojas had it in spades. Other players would send folks like him. Rob wasn't sure that Mac wasn't a better choice to lead this mission, but he didn't think her field skills were up to that side of things, even if her savvy was.

The hatch opened behind him. Mac's perfume preceded her. Roses, but not spring. Fall, just as they are sending out one last *fuck you* to the universe before going to sleep for the winter. Darker and heavier, though he wasn't sure he could compare it to anything he'd know.

He glanced over as she walked up beside him in the space between the two stations, rather than dropping in to sit next to him.

"The mission will start when we hit the ground," she said quietly.

That was one way to interpret it. Technically, it had started when someone sent him a note to come into the office instead of having the day off.

But yeah, things would get serious on the ground.

He studied her face, standing there, looming over him.

"You've got an hour or so before you start your glide in?" she asked.

"Roughly," he nodded. "Got instructions, but space is a little busy around here, so I'm waiting for my allotted slot to land."

She put a hand on his shoulder.

Mac wasn't the kind to touch. She didn't hug, or grasp an elbow when talking. Generally, she was all about personal space. He allowed the surprise to show on his face.

"I've been trying to get deep inside Carlota's mind," she continued.

Rob noted that both she and Alicia never referred to Rojas by her last name. Nor as *Hummingbird*.

Always *Carlota*.

He nodded to prompt her.

"I think I have certain aspects nailed, just based on where I'd have gone, were it me," Mac said next.

Which was exactly why he'd wanted her here. And why she and Alicia gave him an edge he didn't think anybody else playing was smart enough to understand.

She grabbed cloth now, pulling at him a little.

Rob turned his shoulders enough to get a really good look at her.

"I want you to come to bed with me, Rob," Mac instructed him. "Maybe I'm feeling lonely and fragile, but so is she, underneath it all. The brass is all polish with steel underneath. Except that I'm not sure how deep it goes until you get to that hollow spot that she can't fill with anything for long."

Rob wasn't sure what she was saying. And then he was. The powers in *Salonnia* had taken Rojas's identity away from her. Part of her burning them all would be for payback, sure. But another part of it would be to find a way that she could keep herself in the game when she'd been subbed out. When her day was supposed to have been done.

Not every footballer got to run the full match. Sometimes, you brought in someone mid-late just to have fresh legs and eyes when everyone else was starting to tire enough to make mistakes.

The superstars were kept out there. They were supposed to be invincible enough to last, never forcing an error.

Rob checked his autopilot settings. He'd been planning on landing himself, but letting the machines do it would be one more way to look just like anyone else. *Nothing here that stood out, officer.*

He flipped the switch to lock everything in and unbuckled.

Mac stepped back only a little as he rose, then slipped forward until she was pressed up against him.

He'd been through method acting with Roxie before. She liked to play a nymphomaniac when it was necessary, and had used him to get into character once. And nearly killed him in the process.

Mac seemed to be inside…*Carlota*'s mind. And roleplaying out what that woman might be going through.

He let her take his hand and draw him aft. Alicia glanced up from her book as they went by, but didn't say anything, so those two must have planned it out.

Mac pulled him into the cabin they had shared, though they'd never gotten more physical than cuddling on this flight. From the look in her eyes, that was about to change.

She seemed emotionally fragile. That seemed to be the cue she wanted him to pick up on, so he let her lead, watching passively as she slowly stripped herself nude before him, before turning to remove his clothing one step at a time.

In control, at a time when she might not be. Might not have anything left to control.

Just like the image of Carlota she had constructed in her mind.

That woman had invented a game that let her challenge every agent in the galaxy to a mental contest.

Jorge and that gang would have probably eaten her for lunch, but they were mostly retired these days, at least according to the man himself. Several new vids and an album Longbow was touring to support had them off-planet and focused, leaving Handsome Rob and his new crew to step into the breach, as it were.

Rob had seen pictures of Mac when she was still an eighteen-year-old named Esmeralda Morgan. Thirty-four years later she had a few more curves than she had then, but not much. Mostly more muscle tone than the lean, hungry child she'd been, once upon a time.

The need communicated itself silently in her fingertips as she touched him, drew him to her, pushed him to the bed where she lay down beside him and then rolled mostly on top of him as his arms came up around her.

Hungry for touch. That was the thing he felt. Smelled. Tasted.

Was she being Carlota now, or had Mac decided that he would be too busy to make love to her once they landed?

Either way, he came out ahead.

How many men might really understand what they were facing here?

How many men would be able to see what drove a woman like Carlota.?

Or Mac?

8

CARLOTA ROSE LANGUIDLY FROM THE DEPTHS OF A comfortable sleep. The chamber was dim and the hour early, so she stretched some in bed and allowed herself the luxury of waking slowly.

After so many years in the field, such a thing felt almost decadent. Not that nobody was looking to bang on her door and arrest her. They just didn't know where to find her.

Finally, she rose, keying on the light enough to see the rest of her sleeping chamber.

A pair of cufflinks gleamed in brilliant iridium from next to her comm on the nightstand. She'd stolen them from Armand after an amazing night in his cabins before vanishing. Better that way.

Beauty, as they say, was only skin deep, and with the lights off, he'd stopped being the bog troll and turned into a late night radio announcer, seducing her with language and vocabulary before moving on to fingertips.

The man had approached her body like a musician might view their favorite cello, an instrument that would make various harmonies, depending on where and how you touched it.

She'd certainly been thankful that his suite seemed to be soundproofed. Her throat had been raw for two days afterwards.

He made love like he played poker, taking a methodical approach so as to master the topic, leaving nothing to chance. She'd never before thought of herself as a deck of cards to be counted and shuffled, but the memory of that night still left her with a smile a week later.

She showered just as slowly as she'd risen. Pampered herself a little as she got ready, even pausing to slip those stolen cufflinks into her pocket as something of a lucky charm. Certainly, some of his luck had rubbed off on her. William and the other one had gotten themselves crossways with the casino's security and been arrested.

Carlota still wondered if they were spies, or just grifters. Hard to separate the two, at least until endgame.

And Armand had been just as fascinating over a late dinner as he'd been across a felt table. He'd scratched an itch Carlota hadn't even been aware of at the time.

She moved out into the main chamber of her suite slowly and studied things. The door had a bar in addition to the electronic locks, keeping someone outside unless they wished to make a tremendous racket gaining entry.

That was good, as there was an otherwise innocent-looking valise off to one side in a corner, seemingly empty until you went to lift it up, and discovered how much it weighed.

The salon space was for entertaining guests, but she had allowed nobody in except the maid.

There was a kitchenette, which she supposed was for those weirdos who liked to cook while on vacation. Or maybe reheat leftover takeout.

She supposed that such a thing made sense to some people.

Mildly disgusted with the concept, Carlota moved to the office area, a desk with a dedicated land-line and comm system for engaging in video conferences.

Again, she flashed back to William and his associate. Salesmen on first blush, but something deeper had been going on. A wrongness to the man reflected in oddly accented words. The casino's security people had seen fit to follow them, and then have the two arrested, probably about the time Armand had gotten her to the scene of his second seduction, this one taking place over sourdough bread nearly good enough for her to consider breaking in to steal some of the starter. Third, fourth, and fifth seductions had occurred later in the evening, while William and his friend were apparently languishing in a jail cell from the rumors that had circulated later.

Carlota shrugged and addressed herself to the valise, lifting it carefully and carrying it to the desk. It took a few moments to carefully remove the thread holding in a false bottom. Inside lay the rest of the manuscript.

At first, she had considered just saving it to a portable memory stick. Or even renting space on some accessible server where other people kept family pictures. That had its benefits, but making it available electronically meant that someone with sufficient processing power could brute force their way around and find it.

No, she'd typed the whole thing to perfection. Made a paper copy that she carried around, the original draft having been around three hundred pages and marked Volume One, because she could be like that.

Suggesting that it might eventually fill an entire shelf would certainly draw in all the players, giving her a challenge she hadn't faced in more than a decade.

She'd carried it to *Borlait*, then mailed off seven copies of Chapter One. The most fun had been calculating the postage options to make sure it arrived everywhere at the same time, as *St. Legier* and *Ladaux* were the farthest away, but had the most advanced postal systems. *Petron* in *Corynthe* was the slowest, but she'd discounted them for the most part. They were pirates who only barely admitted to being part of a larger political entity, and then only in the last several years after Captain Keller had turned herself into a queen over them. *Lincolnshire's Ramsey* actually was reasonably close to *Ladaux* in *Aquitaine*, in terms of days to expected delivery.

That had left three local copies: her literary agent, her publisher, and the *Salonnian* Intelligence Bureau. All of the previous bundles had gone priority starmail. The Administrator got his copy bulk-class, the proverbial slow boat from China, as people still called it all these millennia later.

And it helped that off-planet post was generally handled by professionals, while *Salonnia* used the system as a patronage source. She'd insured all three and even then knew the odds had been fifty/fifty that they would arrive, let alone on any sort of schedule.

And she certainly couldn't ask for confirmation of delivery without leaving an address.

Certain individuals would be quite upset when they read those contents. Postal system inviolability would be the first thing tossed out the window in their mad quest to find her.

So she could only speculate. But that just added an extra layer of spice to everything else, didn't it, since she could never guess who might be coming after her until they arrived?

Carlota felt more alive than she had in twenty years.

She pulled the remainder of the manuscript out of the hiding place under the false bottom and set the case aside.

The stack of papers took center stage on the desk, minus that effusively incendiary introduction and the chapter where she explained what those cryptic references in the table of contents might mean, working on the assumption that several of her readers might not understand intelligence terms.

Most of them would. That just broadened her smile.

Because she'd invented this game from whole cloth, there were certain rules that had to be followed. At least in her head, which was what really mattered.

She pulled Chapter Three off the stack and set the rest aside, quickly reading through the true beginnings of her narrative. The Early Days, as she liked to think of them, when she was still somewhat innocent, wholly patriotic, and willing to do all manner of things at the behest and orders of those superiors that she had still trusted in those days.

Her libido and creativity had been put to work for her own purposes now, rather than what a fat, old man in a cheap suit back on *Salonnia* itself—the planet, in a low office tower on the northwestern edge of Azgon—had wanted from her.

She was a free agent today, in every sense of the word.

And she would show them.

Working with speed but precision, she returned the rest of the manuscript to the case and sewed the false bottom back in. If they could stop her before she mailed every chapter, they would win. That easy.

If they couldn't, she won. Her agent and a few of the publishers she'd talked to had already been warned that bad men would seek to shut them down before her memoir could see the light of day, and every single one of them had begun to look on that as a challenge.

Carlota might have chosen them for exactly that reason.

She had seven mailing packets she had picked up

yesterday that she withdrew from a nearby drawer and began addressing, with a note on each as to the specifics of class when mailing, so everyone got them at the same time.

The only clue she was leaving everyone was that the envelopes had each originated from *Borlait*, from various postal offices in Bennan, the city at the center of the planet's economy.

After all, how hard could it be to find her in a city of thirty million people, once you included all the resorts and tourists?

She smiled and got to work.

9

Emil walked into the outer office and scowled at the pretty young woman seated behind the desk. He didn't feel old, but realized at a glance that she could be his granddaughter.

He wondered if he'd been in this business for too long.

Certainly, he made an impression on the woman, as she gulped, eyes wide like a fawn.

"May—may I help you, sir?" she finally stammered.

Emil reached into the breast pocket of his old jacket and pulled out a wallet with his identity papers. These even had his real name, something he hadn't used in the field more than a handful of times.

He stepped across the small reception area, smelling the faintest hint of mold in the background, like a smoke on his tongue, and handed the leather-bound container across the countertop to her.

As she opened it to read, he stood with his hands crossed behind his back, studying himself in the faint reflection of a glass-fronted painting behind her on the wall. Short and heavy-set, going back decades. Completely gray, which was relatively new, though the full beard had led the way back when he'd been a mere stripling at forty.

For this mission, he'd dug out his favorite cap, the one that made folks think he was a fishing boat captain, possibly retired, though the blue eyes were still shrewd.

The woman gasped and twitched as the contents of the wallet became clear. How often did the *Fribourg Empire* send a *diplomat* to the offices of a small publishing house without warning? Hardly ever. Doubly so in *Salonnia*.

The papers might say diplomatic service, but the woman stared at him like she knew the truth.

But then, this was not the first time this particular company had gotten their hands on…certain literary events that perhaps should not have seen the light of day.

Emil smiled at her, prompting her as one pretty hand had half started across to the intercom on her desk.

She completed the motion.

"Mr. Constanz?" she said into the handset she held to her ear like a life preserver. "Sir, there's a man to see you. A Mr. Emil Yankov…No, sir…Yes, sir…I think he's a spy."

Emil nodded again. She was brighter than she looked. Or more jaded. He supposed the publishing industry would sour one fairly quickly on human nature.

Still, that would make everything easier for everyone.

She replaced the handset and handed him back the wallet.

"He'll be right up, Mr. Yankov," she said warily.

"Thank you," he nodded, stepping back and finding a spot on one of the two couches he had largely ignored earlier.

Leather. Worn with age and countless bodies scraping across them. Originally a mustard color, perhaps, faded now to something a little more yellow than his Anglo skin. Perhaps what you might find in *Corynthe*, were this office moved wholesale.

The door behind the receptionist opened quickly and a middle-aged progressive liberal male stood there. Once, probably a college radical. Two decades since had introduced him to the realities of the world, but Jan Constanz had only tempered his tendencies, according to all the files *Salonnian* Intelligence kept on the man.

Emil had memorized those yesterday when he arrived on planet.

Constanz scowled when he looked this way. Emil wasn't dressed in a snappy suit and tie. Instead, heavy slacks of a tough canvas in faded tan. White shirt with a standing collar. Jacket rather than a blazer, because he wasn't here to charm you with his wit and fashion sense.

Plus, Constanz wasn't that kind of publisher.

Emil rose and studied the man neutrally.

"*Salonnia*?" Constanz asked.

"*Imperial Fribourg*," Emil replied, placing everything on the battleground up front, in case Constanz had any doubts.

"Let's talk in my office," the man said. "Amy, hold all calls."

Emil followed Constanz back into a warren of desks, cubicles, offices, and stacks of bankers boxes that probably held manuscripts never quite thrown away. Nor important enough to store offsite.

They ended up in an office no larger than the three others along the alleyway leading to it, with the corner seemingly a conference room. Emil noted that facet of the man's personality and took a spot on the clean chair, the other one having been precariously buried under stacks of…things. Paper and books for the most part.

"Jan Constanz."

"Emil Yankov."

"Are you here to shut us down, Yankov?" Constanz began as he sat.

"Not yet," Emil answered.

It cost him nothing to be honest with some of his answers. Fewer miscalculations later that way.

"I presume a spy within my employees?" Constanz nodded.

Emil shrugged.

"Perhaps a *concerned citizen* might be a better nomenclature," he offered. "Someone willing to whisper in certain ears when they saw something that might be a problem."

"I assume you're here about the Rojas manuscript?" Constanz continued.

Emil nodded.

"We have Chapter Three now," the little rabble rouser said with a smile. "Her first decade in the industry, so to speak, when she was largely used as a honeypot to trap enemy agents because her superiors didn't put any faith in the woman's intelligence. From there, certain assassinations and governments overthrown, both *Salonnian* and elsewhere."

Emil shrugged. He already had a low opinion of his *Salonnian* counterparts. Junior partners who were very much junior. And exceptionally sexist, but that was the nature of *Salonnian* culture. *Fribourg* wasn't much better, but perhaps a bit more paternalistic.

Still, Emil had done similar things when he was younger, ordering pretty female agents to fuck their way into position to betray a target later. He himself been ordered to seduce a variety of victims as well.

It was an ugly, soul-crushing line of work if you had any hopes about the nature of humanity.

Fortunately, none of that kept him awake at night.

"So what does Imperial Intelligence wish to communicate?" Constanz asked. "We're within our legal rights to publish the book. And it's not like I'm the only person she's mailing these packets to."

"Understood," Emil agreed, placing things on the chessboard. "And no doubt you will make arrangements to print at a facility somewhere else in secrecy, rather than one of your main ones, against the risk of a warehouse fire destroying everything."

Constanz nodded warily. The man had played all manner of games with the local junior varsity over the last decade or more. He had never had something explosive enough that the Emperor might grow concerned.

This was a larger—and far more dangerous—game.

"What happens if she does not deliver the full manuscript?" Emil inquired.

"Chapter Two is missing three pages," Constanz said, reaching into the pile off to his right and pulling out a thin folder that he handed across the desk to Emil's clutching hands. "Those are the ones that actually name names and provide the sorts of precise details that transform this beyond a case of prosecutable libel. Chapter Three is the same way."

Emil didn't bother to hide his grimace as he flipped through the document, noting the gaps in the numbering.

"And all of the following persons were present at the meeting on August Fourth at Bureau Headquarters in Azgon when the final decisions was made to…"

Yes. Explosive. Careers would be ruined. Syndicates would be materially damaged, because politicians that they owned might be destroyed. Might even be prosecuted, depending.

Much of what intelligence agencies did was generally accepted under unwritten agreements of behavior, but not all of it was fully legal.

And the mob was an unforgiving jury.

He made to hand the folder back.

"That's your copy," Constanz waved him off. "I have been expecting someone to arrive. As to your question, I cannot publish the manuscript until it is complete. You know that. Those gaps open me up to government censure if I tried. Criminal charges sufficient to shut me down for good. However, once I have them, then I will rush it to print. The government might try to suppress, but prior censorship laws favor me, as the oligarchs would rather be able to go after someone for libel and slander than keep them from talking. Better penalties."

"And if they did prevent publication somehow?" Emil asked.

Constanz was sharper than the file suggested. Or better prepared for such a thing.

"You can possibly prevent *Salonnian* publication, Agent Yankov," Constanz laughed. "As noted, she sent it somewhere in *Fribourg*, too. Also *Aquitaine*, *Lincolnshire*, and *Corynthe*, plus who knows where else. I doubt that you can get them all, at which point smugglers will come into play, hauling pallets of books in hidden compartments and selling them like illegal liquors from back alleys."

It was Emil's turn to grimace. *Salonnia* was the galactic hub of smuggling, mostly because the oligarchs and Syndicates liked it that way. And it served *Fribourg's* purposes as well. Not everything needed to be taxed at punishing rates.

He wondered if that perception was going to bite them all in the ass this time.

"Would you be offended if I asked you to keep providing me copies as they came in?" Emil asked grimly.

"If it keeps you folks from breaking in here at night and making a mess of things, that would be the better option," Constanz replied.

Emil nodded and handed the man a business card with local information for *Borlait*.

He wasn't *Salonnian*. The failure of the locals to handle something like this woman wasn't going to reflect on him. Imperial Intelligence had sent Emil to locate the woman behind this mess herself, because she very obviously knew far more about the inner workings of the *Salonnian* Intelligence Bureau than supposed. And knew about things that Emil was fairly certain hadn't been communicated at any point to his superiors on *St. Legier*.

His bosses wanted to capture her so they could know what other information the woman contained.

Failing that, they wanted her eliminated before *Aquitaine* could get to her.

10

────────

Handsome Rob had carefully made three distinct reservations at the hotel while he'd been in orbit. Money had been transferred to three accounts, as though everyone here wanted to get away from each other on the ground, cooped up for too long on a small ship.

Not that they were a team of foreign agents quietly invading *Borlait* as part of the game to track down *Hummingbird*.

Mac was staying upstairs in one of the nicer suites. Not quite penthouse, but spendy and overlarge for a single woman traveling. She didn't really have a legend on this mission, so was playing it open enough to distract everyone from the other two.

Alicia had a simple room like a traveler on vacation. She would handle electronic security, both offense and defense, for the three of them. As well as tracking down anybody Rob could find.

Without access to the local network of agents or stringers, he was flying mostly in the dark, but that wasn't really anything new. Miguel frequently used him in situations where all spy craft had fallen apart and you were reduced to guessing and blunt force.

What the boss occasionally called *kinetic solutions*. The kind of thing where you rattled a box to see what fell out or who responded. While keeping yourself alive in the process.

The term was also used for assassinations occasionally, but those were exceptionally rare in the business, for all that he had such a job title. You were far better off recruiting agents and breaking in someplace to read files when nobody was looking.

It was only when somebody went rogue that you needed the specialized skills. The killers.

Weren't many like him. Wasn't much need for them, which was good.

Carlota Rojas was off the reservation in bad ways, ways that might call such players down on her as she was fleeing across the desert and leaving a trail of dust behind her.

As, hopefully, were the folks chasing her.

Rob had gone back and forth on how he should present for this mission, and finally settled on just being the pilot. That kept him farthest out of the light, while Mac could keep eyes on Carlota when they spotted her. Not that it took much with a woman that beautiful.

He walked across the hotel lobby by himself, having arrived last on purpose. Alicia already owned their reservation system and was working outwards to see what other resources she could tap.

The woman hated being underestimated. This was the same Alicia who had printed her resume on Dillon's personal printer, in his office, at headquarters. The head of the Service's Research and Development Inspectorate, Dillon Vergrue, who had convinced the people heading out to kick in Alicia's door to knock instead.

Then he had gone and hired her.

Rob was turning her into another field agent. Of sorts. He didn't really understand computers, not like she did. And now he didn't have to, as he had a galaxy-class expert handy to do things and explain shit to him.

"Reservation for Segura," he told the young man behind the counter.

"Here you go," the man replied as they handled everything and Roberto Segura got checked in.

It was a little weird, traveling under...well, it wasn't his real name, but it was the one he'd been assigned as a courier, and kept all the way up to the present. A lot of folks called him Handsome Rob, but that was Jorge's fault.

He nodded, collected his things, and headed up to the room. Most of his gear would remain with the ship until he had a better idea what he would need, then he'd get a storage space in town. Alicia needed to identify which ones they could trust with the arsenal of weapons and toys he had brought from *Ramsey*.

Upstairs, Rob deposited his things, then took the stairs up a few stories of the tower to Alicia's room. Mac had come down as well, so they settled in.

Alicia had a device sitting on the coffee table and blinking every three seconds. He'd seen similar ones, but most jammers like that were the size of a cigarillo lighter that would fit inside your fist. Why did you need one that might fit in a 350ml can?

Unless you wanted to disrupt anybody within maybe forty yards.

"So, I have a rough start," Alicia said as Rob settled across from her on the couch with Mac leaned against him.

Alicia had crossed her legs and still somehow fit in a comfortable chair, with a clamshell, traveling computer on her lap, connected to the wall mount rather than relying on radio packets. More stable signal, less likely to be sniffed and maybe hacked.

That much, he understood.

"According to the schedule Carlota suggested when she sent the first packet, she should have mailed Chapter Three by now," Alicia continued. "It ought to have arrived at the local publisher earlier this week. They are here in Bennan."

"Here," Rob grunted with a smile.

"Twenty-eight million inhabitants in the local jurisdiction," Alicia shrugged. "Why isn't she going somewhere else each time? We'd never find her."

"The same reason she didn't just mail the completed manuscript to everyone and watch things catch fire," Mac spoke up, in her role as Carlota's stunt double. Or something. "This is a game, and she has to show them she's better than they are by giving them a chance to stop her. In their failure, she wins."

"And dies," Rob said. "I still don't think any of you have mentally gotten to the point where the finished manuscript is done and ready to be published. Sure, you win, but the agencies aren't going to stop at that point and go back to their locker rooms, just because the time-keeper whistled the end of the game."

"They'll keep coming after us forever," Mac nodded, still half in the mindset of that other woman. "We need to die, and make it look believable."

"And public," he added. "There must be proof that you died."

"They don't have my physical records," Mac said. "According to Carlota, she destroyed those."

"So a female of the right general shape, damaged in death enough that the face is unrecognizable," Rob nodded, watching the two women blink and flinch a little, but they weren't on as personal of terms with death as he was. "I wonder if she has one already, or will need to get such a candidate when she gets closer."

"Has?" Alicia asked.

"We're in a big city," Rob shrugged. "Folks die of a variety of things. The city will have a morgue, and you have a lot of open space on this world to use as a potter's field. *Borlait* isn't completely empty, once you get more than fifty miles from Bennan. It just feels that way because population density falls off to almost nothing. Almost."

"So we need to figure out how she fakes her death?" Mac asked.

"Do you want to die, Carlota?" he asked the woman leaned against him to steal his heat, then turned to include Alicia in his gaze. "All this for that singular blaze of glory? Or did you want to be able to stand off to one side watching and laughing quietly as they poke at the remains of the poor soul they think is you?"

"They don't get to win," Mac growled at him. "Not like that."

"There you go," he nodded. "We need to find the local publisher office or her literary agent, whoever will be easier to break into, so I can see what new things she's included, like additional clues. Then we need to find out how she plans to die."

"So we can help kill her for good?" Alicia asked.

"So we can offer her asylum if she wants it," he countered. "Everybody else will want her dead. Even if she is, somebody might recognize her later. She'll need help to properly vanish."

"I thought you people were experts at assuming new identities," Alicia said. "That's what all the cowboys are always saying to try to impress me."

"Those require a professional depth of detail in various systems to look real," he said. "You two understand better than I do how many places you might pull tidbits from. What happens if you only find a reference in one place?"

"Looks hinky," Mac nodded. "Which causes folks like us to start digging."

"Exactly," he smiled. "So you need someone with government-level powers and money to really put details in a variety of semi-random systems. Credit reports. Rental history. Old traffic tickets. Various social network accounts. Yearbooks. Not many people live such mundane and boring lives that they don't show up in those places, and they leave traces elsewhere."

"So how would you do it?" Mac asked.

She and Alicia had both been in cryptography, which was a highly specialized space filled with mathematics. About as pure and clean as you could get. And as far from getting blood all over your hands as possible and still be in the same building.

"The Service regularly opens new accounts for folks," he grinned. "Starts by registering a birth officially, then put the paperwork in the drawer for several years. Goes back later and insert schooling and vaccination records. Slowly build things up by just leaving messiness. Family. Friends. Cousins. Whatever. Eventually, the records age up to be the same as someone being recruited, and you can swap them in, minus all the things that might let an enemy agent know any sort of truth about them."

"You sound like an expert," Mac observed.

"I wasn't born as Roberto Segura," he replied with a grim smile. "That came much later. Usually with couriers that they expect to have a long career with the Service."

"What about Jorge?" Mac asked.

"That's his real name, as far as I know," Rob said. "He was once a serious thespian doing dramatic work. Then that one screwball comedy to pay some bills and he was suddenly typecast and famous. However, instead of railing against it and fighting to get back to the serious stuff, he just started making low-budget action comedies that took advantage of his reputation and made him filthy, stinking rich. After a while, he got so famous for that phase of his career that he could do things for the Service and nobody would ever believe that the man was really a spy. Look at some of the crazy shit he got me into, after all."

"I still think a lot of that stuff was made up," Alicia interjected.

"Worse," Rob turned to her and smiled. "We had to leave out some of the crazier bits from the official report because Miguel would never believe it."

"Such as?"

"We really did recruit a group of mercenary soldiers to attack that one pirate base," he said soberly. "They thought that they were making a movie, right up until five minutes before we dropped when Jorge told them the truth and started handing out real weapons. Mrs. Jones led a team of killers across the surface of a small, atmosphere-free moon, with live firepower. And she got the high score. Longbow, of all people, had the second most kills that day."

Both women kind of sat there stunned.

Every once in a while, the truth was bigger than anybody would believe of any video fantasy.

"Alicia, find me morgues and other places where we might find or hide a body," he instructed the woman.

"Hide?"

"You haven't gotten that far ahead in your thinking as Carlota," he said. "I'm betting she hasn't, either. Maybe we can find her and give her an opportunity to save her own life. If not, we can be sitting close by like a spider when she finally figures it out and starts to run."

"Okay," Alicia replied quietly. "What else?"

"Get me the publisher and the agent," he said. "I'll handle the breaking and entering."

"What about me?" Mac asked.

"We don't know what she looks like, beyond a few, basic statistics," Rob grinned. "I'm willing to bet that others are in the same boat. You pretend to be rich, semi-famous, and interesting. I mean more than usual. Let's see if any enemy agents start sniffing around and we can blow their covers. Miguel sent me here primarily to damage other agencies. Losing their people because someone got arrested or got their face on the morning newssheet works in our favor."

Mac grinned at him. She was already being Carlota in her head. He could see the woman becoming something of a stunt double for the woman, like Roxy had secretly been for Mrs. Jones in the old days.

He was, after all, here to create chaos. What better way to do it?

11

MAC HAD BEEN AT THE TOP OF HER CLASS OF FIELD agents for all the mental stuff. Having several advanced degrees in mathematics and related fields helped. And she'd trained just as hard as the younger candidates did on the physical side of things, coming in top third among men and women twenty and thirty years her junior.

It was only when she started measuring herself against Handsome that she felt bad, but he had been specifically groomed, recruited, and trained to transform into the man he was. She had woken up one morning and didn't want to be a numbers nerd anymore.

Mac was happy to admit that almost any other boss besides Miguel Cabrill wouldn't have let her have this kind of mid-life crisis and reinvent herself. Hell, this was the very thing that Carlota hadn't been allowed to do.

Put out to pasture, because men thought that women were too old to be sexy after twenty-seven. Not that she still harbored resentment at Umberto for running off with a waitress because a smarter wife was more than he could handle.

He'd expected her to be quiet, pliant, and vapid. Certainly, that's what he'd married, the second time around.

Mac had never married again. Had dated, but never found a man or woman who drew her like a moth to a flame. She'd been busy proving that a former fashion model, however accidental, could be a brilliant mathematician named Esmeralda MacTavish.

Mac had only come along later. Mid-life crisis and all that.

She sat in the bar at one of the local resort casinos and drank something floofy and long on juice instead of alcohol. Rob drank staggering amounts regularly, but that was training his liver to be able to drink anybody under the table. And he had pills he could take that caused a lot of the alcohol to pass straight through without being absorbed, if he had sufficient warning.

With her dyed hair, she was portraying a possibly lonely woman in her early forties without much to do except sit in bars and look stunning. She could still wear the same pants she'd done at twenty. It was the shoulders, lats, and breasts that had gotten bigger and wider over time.

She spent effort on machines to give her muscles. Menopause had caused her chest to…expand. Men and women alike seemed to appreciate it, as they stared often enough.

Tonight, she had poured herself into a sleek, silver sheath that made her look like a sword, with her dark blond hair up in a tail that left her shoulders bare and showed off her tan. She'd worked hard on the tan on the way here, getting everything perfectly smooth, in case she needed to show it off.

Not many men other than Rob had seen her nude. Nor touched her. None, really, other than a few flings in the five years or so before Rob stepped into her life as something of a…partner. However you wanted to quantify their relationship.

Dinner infrequently, back at *Ramsey* when both of them might be in town. Never more than that. The afternoon in orbit, just before landing, had been the first time they'd laid together in nearly a year. Since *Shravishtha Prime* and a mission that had called for it at the time to maintain their legends against enemy spies.

Did Carlota have anybody that might understand the need for touch, when you still wanted them to go away after cooking you breakfast in the morning?

So many questions she wanted to ask the woman, comparing her to the image Mac had crafted in her mind.

Tonight, she was bait. And a special kind, since the right people wouldn't really want her, once they got close enough to determine that she wasn't Carlota. If they could. Mac had a stunner tucked away in the folds of her dress where she could get at it quickly if she needed, plus the Service had required her to study unarmed forms of combat. Mostly softer versions of Kung Fu that focused on eluding combat rather than punching.

Her instructor referred to it as old people prison fighting. Where you didn't have time for all that silliness, so you just wanted to knock someone down long enough that you could run away.

Or sidestep and throw them into traffic and let a bus hit them instead.

She sipped her drink and put out pheromones tonight. The bar itself wasn't packed, but it was doing a brisk business. She was here to be seen. Noticed.

Hopefully, not touched. She could get that elsewhere if she needed it.

Carlota would be jealous. Would that be enough to bring her out of the woodwork, too?

12

_____

ROB WAS EIGHTEEN STORIES UP, ON A ROOF LOOKING down.

He liked out-thinking his opponents. Made things way more interesting, when you could get them to do most of the work for you.

Unfortunately, that wasn't going to be much of an option here. He had a blank canvas and a full spectrum of paint, plus an unknown number of potential witnesses.

So he was back to kinetic solutions. Physical force instead of elegance. Good thing Miguel had sent an expert.

His target was Carlota's publisher on _Borlait_. They'd considered the literary agent, but Rob assumed that the woman was smart enough to hide the manuscript someplace safe, rather than carrying it around with her, legal niceties notwithstanding. Too easy for someone to steal it from a one-lawyer office, or break into her flat for it.

The publisher, on the other hand, would have the tools to make a hundred copies and stash them wherever. Plus, Alicia had assured him that security around the office was poor.

Almost negligible, but he had to account for the fact that it was probably meant to keep the merely mortal out.

Not Alicia.

Rob studied the building from the top of the taller building across the alley.

Office tower. Fourteen stories tall. Lower middle kind of place, filled with lawyers, shippers, salespeople. And one publishing house.

Folks not normally important enough to really bother with, when there were a few towers in sight where a single corporation might fill all thirty or fifty stories with folks. Usually the ones handling back-office tasks for a resort, from HR to PR to kitchen supplies.

Logistics was a complicated skill set. Without a full planet to draw on, a lot of things had to be shipped in from elsewhere, but that just meant that much of *Borlait* was a game preserve for rich tourists to explore.

Bennan was the heart and soul of the planet, but even a rich place like this had a few wrong neighborhoods.

The city had street lights, but most of them were ground-level for pedestrians and vehicles. Rob had circled the building four times over the course of the day, another tourist going from A to B and a little lost.

He was pretty sure nobody had recognized him for what he was, but the two people he had seen that stood out were both looking for a woman in her early fifties.

Why they might think that Carlota would come to the publisher directly was anybody's guess, but Rob supposed that if you had pulled in every single body you could, including local law enforcement, then you could afford to just watch the building. And maybe they were watching for folks like him, latecomers to the party that they could watch or maybe arrest.

Which was why he was on the roof. Too easy to be

spotted on the ground, if he tried to enter a dark office tower after hours. Alarms would sound, but more importantly, eyeballs would notice and he'd have other issues.

Once upon a time, Nigel Phipps had been a cowboy with *Aquitaine*'s Fourth Saxon Legion, before they'd gotten famous. Hussars in the galactic age, except that Keller had shown just how dangerous such a concept could be.

Nigel had retired before then, though, hooking up with Jorge and the *Can't Shoot Straight Gang* as their armorer and weapons specialist. He'd come up with some really weird ideas for low-tech toys, and made sure that Rob carried them in the field.

He'd also saved Rob's ass with such requirements, that one morning somebody had tried to kick in Rob's front door to shoot him, back on *Ramsey*.

Tonight, a climbing harness. You could do this with repulsers, but they made noise and tended to flash lights downward, which would be exactly wrong, since the folks he wanted to avoid were all below him.

Nigel would be pleased, next time Rob saw him and could describe this situation.

The roof over there was almost certainly locked and alarmed. Maybe something he could disable, but maybe not. Alicia had gotten inside the building's wiring, and assured him that it was a mechanical system, rather than centrally controlled from a single switch she could commandeer.

Funny that something could be so cheap and simple that it defeated the most powerful computer hackers out there. Doubly so when it was accidental, rather than someone making conscious decisions.

Cutting the power to the building would also cut the alarms, but that might set off alarms downtown at the power company, who would send someone to investigate. Probably police but maybe fire as well, just in case.

Instead, Rob had sat in a nearby coffee shop that afternoon and noted that the building didn't have central cooling. The climate of Bennan was as close to perfect as you could get, so they might not have ever bothered.

That meant windows open, sometimes facing out onto fire escapes. Sometimes, patios. Sometimes just open.

Not everyone had closed them before they went home tonight.

Rob nodded and pulled out a nightvision rig that he hooked over his head, ocular still up, but available when he needed it. Next, he pulled a crossbow and a thing Nigel had invented in his spare time.

Two electric pulley wheels. Rob peeled the backing off one and stuck it right to the side of the building he was on. He pulled a cord out of the bag and attached it to the pulley.

The bolt he loaded into the crossbow held the other end of the rope, with a warhead that would hit, rupture, and then goop itself against the wall over there in the blink of an eye. Both ends were rated for over one thousand kilograms, as long as the walls they were attached to didn't rupture.

He turned back and spied his target, a window second floor down from the top, where they had a patio about twelve feet wide with a charcoal grill, a fern in a pot, and a chair.

Rob lined up the shot and fired with a dull thwap as the rope uncoiled.

Thud. Squish.

He counted to three and set the crossbow down, picking up the line and drawing it tight before clamping it off. Now, he had a loop that connected both buildings. About a thirty degree slant, but he'd climbed with worse.

Patiently, Rob broke down the crossbow and other gear and put it all away. He slung the backpack and attached his climbing harness to the loop, checked everything by pulling as hard as he could, then climbed over the coping and lowered himself.

Hanging from the pullies, he set the electric motor to slowly lower him across the alley like a gondola, watching below where anybody might happen to be looking at the night sky as he crossed, and ahead, in case somebody suddenly appeared at a nearby window, where he would no doubt look silly as he came towards them, a giant black owl hunting.

Nothing.

The watchers he thought were plainclothes cops were almost diagonal away from him, and the pair he'd marked as stringers for some other agency were busy not being seen by the cops.

Rob crossed until he was above the patio and stopped the motor. He'd gotten the spacing just about perfect, so he was able to stand on the rail and hold the loop with one hand as he unhooked everything.

Rather than jump down and make any noise, he let patience be his byword and squatted, shifting his hands and moving like warm molasses.

The window was open. The space inside dark, but that dark you got in offices, where there were always minimal lights and emergency markers. Not enough to read by, but more than enough to make out empty desks, filing cabinets, and office doors open like mouths.

Rob reached into a pocket and pulled out one of Alicia's hand scanners, pointing it at the open sill first and making sure there weren't any defensive lasers or something. Satisfied, he pointed it deeper inside. This was an insurance processing company, where they got claims for workers comp and sent out investigators to handle things. Not a government agency, but a government contract, because the biggest employers around here were the resorts, and they were forever dealing with injuries on the job.

Nature of the business, he'd been given to understand.

And the resorts didn't want to pay out any more than they had to, so this place had enough funding to really investigate. However, not enough to be a problem that might bite the hand that fed it.

Couldn't have that.

He looked around once. He didn't see anybody in the alley below or looking over the roof two stories above him, so Rob folded himself in half and climbed in.

Inside, relatively wide corridors between clusters of desks crammed together. He supposed field operatives would carry clamshells with them everywhere, so they just needed a flat surface to work and a comm to chat on.

Not a lot of equipment overhead. Spares tucked in a storage room somewhere with proper security, but he didn't need any of that.

Instead, he lowered the nightvision and pulled a stunner from his pocket. Just enough to knock somebody down without hurting them, because if he had to use it, this part of the mission was blown and he'd be in flight mode away from enemy agents desperately interested in identifying him, same as he was trying to do to them.

Hopefully, Alicia had been able to break into some of the street cameras around here, so he could point to specific places and she could pull images of those faces for Miguel.

Rob made it to the front door. Outside, he could see a spot for a keycard to be held up on the sidewall and the glass doors would unlock. Inside, he presumed a radar sensor would spot him approaching and unlock things with a click. That was pretty standard design.

He also noted the gap between the double doors. Not

much. Maybe a centimeter clearance. Sufficient that you could stick your pinky through, but not much more.

He didn't need more.

With the ocular down, his face was hidden and his gloves would prevent fingerprints. Someone might notice the door opening late at night, but they might not. At least not for a while if he was lucky. And any cameras that might see him would only see a faceless figure in black.

He approached the door sensors slowly and heard the click.

Rob smiled and pushed them open, heading out into the hallway and looking right and left for the stairwell as the doors clicked again and swung shut to lock.

For now.

He took the stairs down to his target slowly, moving on silent feet. The stairwells had sensors that registered movement and lit up, so he left the ocular in place and just turned it all the way down.

Exiting the stairs, he was again in dimness, so he dialed up the night vision. No guards in this building that might need to move around, so he shouldn't run into anybody, and all of the offices windows had been dark before he started this.

The publisher had a wooden door with a glass window that was frosted over and painted with the corporate name. Worse, they had mechanical locks. As in, metal keys with teeth that turned.

Rob grinned as he knelt and started to work. Nothing fancy, as with the rest of the building. Four pins and it took him less than twenty seconds to have it open. He slipped inside and closed the door behind him, setting the lock just in case somebody came along while he was inside and maybe giving him that much warning.

Receptionist's office. Two couches and a chair. Low

counter with workspace behind it. Potted plants in two corners. Cheap reproduction artwork framed on two walls. Door behind him. Door deeper in.

Rob opened the far door and entered what he could only classify as a maze.

Fortunately, Alicia had gotten her hands on the original blueprints, as well as the as-built results, so he knew which office belonged to Jan Constanz, Publisher, Constanz Books.

Rob was certain he'd have never found it otherwise. The spaces were crammed with boxes that narrowed things down to the point the fire marshal must have been taking bribes under the table. Or just never came and inspected the place. There was always that.

Small offices. Lots of them, all crammed with books and boxes. It was almost like a college, with all the professors lined up in their little kingdoms.

Rob counted down and found his target. Constanz didn't have a window, which was weird, but Rob supposed that not everybody wanted a view. And all you would see would be another building nearby, as this was the shortest building in the area.

Not much sun.

He paused at the door and looked slowly around with the ocular cranked, but nothing moved. Satisfied, he turned it off and lifted it to his forehead, moving to the desk and turning on a lamp.

The usual mess. Stacks of manuscripts, files, and detritus semi-organized. One coffee mug that might be growing a new civilization in the bottom from the smell of the sludge.

Next to it, Rob couldn't help but whistle to himself as his brain engaged on the letters his eyes had picked up.

Emil Yankov. Imperial Intelligence. And a number to call.

Rob really wanted to steal the card. It might even have a

fingerprint on it that he could lift, which would do wonders. Nobody, however, needed to know that he'd been here.

Pity. Maybe Nigel needed to invent some sort of tool that could secretly lift fingerprints? Cops might have such a thing, but why would they need it to be fast and secret? Why would anybody?

Other than someone like him, committing breaking and entering.

He pulled a camera and snapped a picture, front and back, before replacing the card exactly as it had been.

Nearby, he found a folder marked Rojas. Rob was careful to pull it, open it, and take images of each page before returning it to the pile. Sure enough, Chapter Three.

He wondered if there was a way he could get on Carlota's mailing list. Breaking in here every few weeks would get silly. And risky. This Yankov fellow had obviously just walked in the front door and requested copies, but Rob didn't feel like tangling with big time players.

Not without a damned good reason, anyway. More than he had at present.

Looking around briefly, nothing else seemed important. Rob checked the usual places where somebody might hide something, but Constanz didn't have any interesting secrets. Nothing blackmailable, at least.

Everybody had secrets. Most of them just weren't worth enough to matter.

He did check the paper calendar on the desk and noted that dates with Carlota Rojas's name written down had been originally marked in pen, and then crossed out, though he wasn't sure why.

He went back to the most recent cover letter, rather than waiting until he got safely away to look at his images.

Shit. Speeding up the game? Every two weeks now, then weekly after seven? That certainly put a hard timer on the end of the game. Other players had just lost more than half the time they'd probably originally expected to have, in order to find Carlota.

Was she feeling the pinch? Or putting the pinch on?

He'd have to ask his two experts when he got back to the hotel. This felt important, but Rob was pretty certain that his gender would get in the way of guessing the correct answer.

He put everything away. Triple checked that it looked normal. Withdrew.

Back in the reception room, he set the front door lock and slipped out, then into the stairwell and up, getting back to the floor where he'd originally entered the building

This was when a crazy-ass redneck like Nigel had gotten inside Rob's head. When Rob had actually started to think like Nigel, and how that man would solve certain problems.

From his pack, he pulled a telescoping piece of metal and attached an unfolded piece of card stock, like a flag. Both slipped between the glass doors easily enough, then Rob lifted them up and turned them ninety degrees.

The inside door sensors were dumb. They registered all this as a person approaching the door from deeper in, and unlocked. Rob pulled the door open and slipped in, disassembling everything as he walked with a smile.

You'd have to watch the footage to make sense of the door opening twice from the inside sensors. Both times, a man in black with no face; once going, once returning.

He made it to the window, clearing everything inside, then outside. Out onto the patio without opening the secured door off to one side, he inspected his rope. Everything good.

Rob climbed up on the wall and attached himself to the rope. Settled, then winched himself back up to the other roof, the electric motors making a little more noise as they had to lift his weight.

Once across the alley, he reached up and caught the coping, pulling himself up and onto the roof as quietly as possible, alert for someone hiding and waiting, but nobody jumped out. He detached himself, then unhooked the rope clamp, pulling it back.

Finally, he detached this pulley with a liquid that broke the adhesive. Nothing he could do at the other end but leave it there and hope nobody figured out what it was for a while. Not that it would be obvious. Folks might think it was part of the building hardware they'd missed previously.

Nobody should connect it with someone breaking into a publisher's office to look around.

Rob packed everything up and went to the stairs going down. He would descend, pop out a fire escape on the far side, and vanish into the night.

The game was speeding up.

Did he have enough time to make all this effort worth it?

13

————

CARLOTA SMILED AS SHE PULLED OUT CHAPTER FOUR
from the valise and put everything back. Hopefully,
everybody was having a small heart attack at the new
schedule. She'd felt like they weren't working all that hard,
since William was the last person who'd made any impression
on her as possibly being trouble. And then Armand had seen
to destroying the man. And that merely as a way to
seduce her.

She thought about the bog troll occasionally, but didn't
go looking.

He might be deep cover for someone and had just been
picking off the competition.

Instead, she'd upped her own personal surveillance.
Paranoia. Whatever you wanted to call it.

She had never returned to that casino where she'd met
Armand and cleaned out everyone else. Not even been on
that resort's property again. Anyone looking might expect her
to return to the scene of the crime, as it were. She would not.

At the same time, sitting in her hotel room passively

waiting for meals, sleep, and the next mailing would drive her to begin chewing on the scenery pretty quickly, so she did get out occasionally.

Just to be a shit, she often put on something of a disguise in order to go into Bennan proper. The town frequently played second fiddle to all of the resorts, but those places paid well, so that money got circulated here because employees never lived on property. That, in turn, meant nice restaurants, plus some civilized comforts, including a symphony as well as several small theaters where folks hoping to break in at one of the resorts auditioned.

Or just put on weird black-box things where a good audience might be fifty people instead of ten thousand, like when some major recording artist did a short residence at a resort for a season.

Tonight, she'd treated herself to weird. Deeply weird.

Humans had first gone into space some ten thousand years ago, back when the planet *Earth* was a place, rather than a burned-out cinder. In all that time, nobody had ever found any intelligent life, other than the evil robots mankind had created.

That didn't stop dreamers from envisioning finding someone, just around the next corner. Perhaps they'd all died off millions of years ago and vanished, only to be awakened somehow today.

At least that was the underlying theme of the musical she'd wandered into, after dinner in a place that was positively a dive. She'd seen the playbill tacked on a community board and it had utterly intrigued her.

Something new, when Carlota had been pretty certain in her cynicism that she'd seen it all.

Singing aliens with tentacles for mouths was new. She couldn't say they were great, but that was the writer. The cast was putting their heart and soul into the performance, and that was enough for the eighteen other folks in the audience with Carlota.

They took a break for an intermission. Carlota went out to the lobby with the others for a glass of wine, and to throw a handful of cedis into a jar to help support the little non-profit running the space.

They dreamed. She'd almost forgotten what that was like. Over a glass of wine, she studied a few cast and crew mingling with almost as many pedestrians, some of whom looked like they'd accidentally wandered into the wrong building.

At the same time, some person had had an idea for a musical about an alien invasion, and convinced enough friends and fellow lunatics to help them put it on. Carlota couldn't see something like this ever playing on one of the big stages at a resort, but she supposed that you had to try. She understood that concept at a deeply visceral level.

Most of the others around her were kids. She could say that. None looked over thirty, save for one woman who had the air of a widow. She was elegant, wearing baggy, straight-leg pants in a chocolate brown, with a snug white shirt and sand-colored vest. Long, blondish hair braided expertly.

Like Carlota, she seemed to be just milling about. Not here with anybody. Not on any timeline to do things.

Waiting for others to arrive, which had been the hallmark of much of Carlota's career. Waiting for agents. Bumping into them briefly to mark them or hand off a note. Or walking away when it didn't feel right, so you could begin assessing fallbacks.

Carlota caught her eye across the space. The woman was tall, even before she'd added those heels. They toasted each other with wine glasses, and the stranger took that as an invitation.

Was it? Carlota wasn't sure. The last thirty years had been

dedicated to doing what she was told, while subsuming herself into roles dictated by others.

That she got to choose the roles these days really didn't change the shape.

Just the level of control she got to exercise. The woman approached carefully, as if uncertain about Carlota's intentions.

Did she have intentions? Armand had been a happy accident. A book that one should never judge by the cover. Few men utterly relished the thought of going down on a woman, which just showed what fools they all were.

The stranger getting closer was utterly gorgeous. Slender, but built with muscles. Bright, blue eyes that probably turned gray in bright sun. Made up to appear younger than she was, which Carlota nodded at. They might be of an age, single women in their early fifties, if you looked at the hands and the corners of the eyes with the right sort of vision.

There were only so many tricks you could play with makeup before you had to visit a professional surgeon and hope that they were also an artist.

Carlota had considered having proper work done to become a stranger, but that would have taken her out of the game for as much as a year, at that moment when the siren call of the manuscript had pulled her out of her depression and given her a reason to fight back. To live.

Would she do it when all this was done?

Carlota had a start when she realized that she'd gotten so wrapped up in her game that she hadn't made it past that day when she was able to walk into a bookstore somewhere and pick up a copy with her name on the cover.

"Is everything okay?" the stranger asked, drawing Carlota back up from squirreling in on herself.

"Sorry," Carlota said. "A random connection in my head

distracted me and reminded me of something I needed to do tomorrow. Or next week."

"I understand those," this gorgeous woman nodded. Even her voice was lovely, as was the hint of jasmine in her perfume. "There are times when it just feels like you are waiting around for someone else to decide to do something. Or not."

Carlota nodded. This was a woman who had that maturity that only a lot of light-years could give you. Youngsters still thought that they could change the galaxy. Could make a difference.

At some point, you realized that all you could change was yourself.

"Or not," Carlota chucked. "Helen."

It was as good a name as any. And not like anyone could track her.

"Erika," the blond replied. "Enjoying the show?"

"More than I expected," Carlota smiled. "Although, truth be told, I wasn't sure what awaited me."

"I know the feeling," Erika replied with a matching grin. "I saw the playbill on a light pole after lunch, and I'm not sure what drew me to it, but it looked just so outrageous that I needed to see for myself."

"Are you staying in Bennan, then?" Carlota asked, a bit surprised, because the resorts existed to keep you on their property and filter away all your money. Getting into town wasn't impossible, as they had to have trams for employees, but still.

"It seemed more interesting," Erika shrugged. "After a while, those resorts all take on a sort of smoothness that fades into the background. I wanted something more intriguing this trip, though I'm not sure what I was looking for. Maybe singing squidfolk."

Carlota joined her in a chuckle. Youngsters thought they knew what they wanted. Rarely did they. Or if they achieved it, it turned out to be fool's gold.

She was something of an expert on the topic.

They made small talk. Carlota found the woman endlessly compelling. Had her husband really run off with a waitress and left someone this smart and beautiful behind?

But then she thought back to the Administrator of the Bureau, patting her on the head because she was past her time and should really just shut up and work at her little desk, or go ahead and resign so they didn't have to listen to her bitching.

"Men are fools, aren't they?" Carlota asked.

Erika nodded in sympathy. It was a girl thing.

"Attention, everyone," a blue squidperson appeared and called. "Intermission will be over shortly, if you could hit the restroom and find your way back to your chairs in five minutes, we'll be ready for Act Two."

Carlota and Erika both made their way to the fresher, smiling as they applied lipstick side by side in the mirror. Tall, elegant, beautiful, smart. Armand, without even the bog troll parts.

Carlota leaned into Erika's shoulder as they crossed back to the auditorium. She even took the woman's hand, feeling Erika squeeze it in return.

"I'll follow you," Carlota said, letting Erika lead her to where the woman had been before. The seats were only two rows, right up against the open space pretending to be a stage, so sitting in the back row and necking with the woman would be poor form.

Still, she leaned over and kissed Erika on the cheek as they sat. Watched the woman's surprise turn to interest. Erika pulled her into a second kiss, but broke away before they got too involved.

Carlota settled and found herself holding hands with the woman. And thinking about Armand and his radio voice.

14

MAC HAD POSITIVELY NOT INTENDED TO GET SEDUCED while she was on this mission. Even Rob had largely kept his emotional distance, beyond going to sleep curled up against her back with one hand around her cupping a breast lightly.

Helen had struck her as the sort of social widow Mac was, though never apparently married to anything except a job she had successfully escaped from.

They sat, holding hands and leaning against each other across the arm rest, listening to a mad scientist aria about the joys of destructive firepower. It really was a silly play, but the three main actors had gone at it like the Lincoln Shakespeare Company, back on *Ramsey*.

She could honor that. It was what came after that she found herself considering with most of her attention, blue tentacles notwithstanding.

Currently, Mac had no itinerary, save to be on call to support Rob and Alicia, both of whom had taken the night off to relax. Rob had reminded her that this was the longest of long surveillance operations, intended to flush out villains.

Instead, she'd stumbled into the most fascinating woman.

Someone her age, but not withered and withdrawn. Vibrant. Sexy. Possibly a little horny, based on that kiss they'd shared before the lights went down.

Did she take the stranger back to her hotel later, possibly after a nightcap? It wasn't that far of a walk, through a nicer part of town. Even with weird warehouses converted to playhouses.

There was nothing in her room that would compromise her. Every bit of secret gear was down with Alicia or back on the ship against future need, so Helen wouldn't accidentally blow her cover if they did end up sleeping together.

The woman was hungry for touch. *That* Mac understood extremely well. Rob was a gentleman because Mrs. Jones had specifically trained him to appreciate an older woman. Most men were unfortunately like Umberto, wanting young, dumb, and busty. They didn't want someone who could provide stimulating conversation, let alone be smarter than them.

Somehow that emasculated them, for reasons Mac had never understood. Maybe she needed to corner Jorge Royo one of these days, and demand answers from him. He was something of a guru on the topic, and he didn't limit himself to bimbos young enough to be his granddaughters.

What was it that Rob had said, quoting the man?

Every woman is as beautiful as she decides to be when she wakes up in the morning.

Helen had chosen to be beautiful today. Mac understood that. It was something of a constant battle, not to give in to the entropy of being over fifty and letting things slide.

Doubly so because she was living on borrowed time. One of these days, Miguel would be replaced, and the new Director would take one look at her previous record and demand changes in her career.

Mac needed to grab life by the scruff of the neck and

bleed it for every bit of excitement and fun she could, while she had the chance.

She leaned over and kissed Helen on the cheek suddenly, surprising the woman. It felt good.

Around them, the final battle rose to stupendous, if silly heights, with the piano player really giving it her all to the point that Mac wondered if the instrument might need to be retuned after this.

Ray guns flashed. Spotlights strobed with the music, presumably replicating explosions. Blue-faced squidpeople cried out in agony and collapsed at the feet of the heroic scientist and his bad-ass assassin wife, who kissed while standing atop a pile of alien corpses.

Very, very silly.

But heartfelt. Close your eyes to the scene and listen to the voices and they were living and dying up there. Helen squeezed her hand and lowered her head on Mac's shoulder.

The woman had chosen to be beautiful this morning. With clinical eyes, Mac would have said a little plain. Nose slightly crooked. Eyes a little wider than perfect.

Suitably average, but a little above average. Cute, but not memorable. Smart, but hiding it behind a façade of *bonhomie* and pleasantness.

Mac started. That described the standard field agent that every agency in the galaxy tried to recruit. Folks who could walk away and be nearly impossible to describe, because so little about them stood out physically. At the same time, the smarter the better. Mac wasn't the only PhD in Mathematics in the building, though none of the others ever completed her level of field training.

Still, an undergraduate degree was a dead minimum for recruitment, followed up with a year of hard training and constant learning for the rest of your life.

To come up with a cipher. Like the woman previously

leaned against her shoulder and now looking at her with a little concern as the lights came up.

"A little overwhelmed there," Mac muttered to her as the score of fans began clapping and hooting, along with the cast and crew. "Tonight was kind of magical."

"I agree," Helen said, leaned slightly in so they touched arms.

Finally, things fell to silence and everybody began making their various ways. There was no backstage, so the cast milled and filed out into the front room where there was more wine and camaraderie to be had.

Mac followed Helen, watching the way the woman moved. It reminded her of Rob, but that might be nothing.

Or *everything*.

Was this somehow Carlota? Or had one of the other agencies somehow been smart enough to catch a clue and also send along a woman of the right age and temperament to get inside Carlota's head?

Except that Rob had pointed out more than once that she and Mrs. Jones were almost unique in the industry of field agents. Partly, that was longevity, as few such folks remained healthy and unknown for that many decades.

And, she had to admit, most women didn't want to work that hard to be available as a sex goddess to tempt younger agents.

Fools, but she wasn't going to change the world herself. She just had to set the kind of example that made it easier for the next woman coming along. Mac had no doubts that having Mrs. Jones as an example of sexy and deadly had worked in her favor when convincing Miguel.

They each bought another glass of pedestrian wine and found a quietish corner where they could face in and keep the rest of the crowd at a social distance.

Mac studied Helen's face, wondering if this was the

infamous *Hummingbird*. And if seducing the woman would work, or allowing herself to be seduced by her.

Helen was standing closer than most women would with a stranger. A hand came out and touched Mac's arm. Obviously, she wasn't the only one thinking such thoughts.

"So now what?" Helen asked.

"Trying to decide if I should invite you to dinner at some all-night diner nearby," Mac said. "Or just skip that part and take you home and have you for dinner. We could always order room service later."

Those brown eyes lit up for a moment. Yes, this was a woman who didn't get cat-called or wolf-whistled as she walked down the street. Never got appreciated by strangers or friends for being *sexy*.

A woman wanted to be noticed. *You just keep your grubby mitts over there until I invite you to touch.*

Mac leaned down some and they were kissing again. Lips, but not hands. Not yet. Wine glasses carefully held off to the sides. Pure lust, but the kind driven by need and an expectation of touch that might require hours to cover all the options, rather than two pumps and a snoring lout beside you on the bed.

Not that she had a low opinion of many men her age. Or younger.

Rob had certainly spoiled her. She'd occasionally considered demanding that Royo take her to bed so he could show her how much of that man's legend held up in the light of day.

Tonight, Helen seemed to be in the same boat. Awakened by the need for tender touch. Open minded enough to take pleasure where she found it.

Seducible.

"Room service would be acceptable," Helen murmured.

Mac turned and found a flat surface to put her wine glass

on. She smiled expectantly at Helen and the woman joined her. They grabbed hands and grinned.

"That wine wasn't that good," Mac said. "I can get us something much better at the hotel. And some first-rate chocolate to pair with it."

Again, those eyes flashed with excitement. Possibly lust.

If this wasn't Carlota, Mac would at least have the pleasure of enjoying the woman and exploring her needs.

But what if it was her elusive quarry?

Then what?

15

CARLOTA HELD ERIKA'S HAND AS THEY WALKED through downtown Bennan, feeling like a naughty schoolgirl sneaking out after curfew. It was such an alien thing that she wondered if she'd been kidnapped and replaced with an impostor.

Or worse, this might be the woman she could have grown up to be, but for everything that came in between. Like Armand, Erika had hidden depths. Unlike the bog troll, she was utterly stunning to behold and tasted like peppermint oil when kissed.

Instead of holding hands and possibly watching the sly looks from folks as they passed, Carlota hooked elbows with the taller woman, two teenage kids skipping school for an afternoon of fun.

Carlota found herself smiling. Laughing even as Erika knew some hilariously rude dirty jokes.

Quickly, they reached the hotel. Carlota had not let her paranoia slip, even as she considered tasting the woman next to her. Bennan was a huge city. Pedestrian traffic even this late at night was fairly heavy.

Partly, that was the impact of the various resorts, who never really slept. You had people coming and going at all hours of the clock, and the ones who lived in town had lives separate from that.

Restaurants either kept to specific meal times, or just stayed open forever, depending. Good ones survived. Bad ones failed and some other kid with a dream gave it a go.

Erika was staying at one of the nicer spots. Not the fanciest or most expensive. If you were going to do that, you might as well stay at a resort.

No, this was a traveler who had money, and understood how to use it. Alone, most of the time, but not lonely. Except on those nights when certain physical needs might suddenly rise up and threaten to overwhelm you.

Carlota pinned Erika against the side of the elevator once the door closed and kissed her hard. With promise.

With need.

Erika returned it with equal fervor, something that few men would understand. Or younger women.

They rode nearly to the top of the tower, intertwined in a way that anyone watching on the security cameras was getting a bit of a free show. Nothing tawdry. Just two women necking profusely.

Few twenty-year-olds knew how to kiss.

Carlota was enjoying herself as Helen. That was strange, in a delightful way. They ended up seated at both ends of a couch, turned inwards with knees and hands touching, but far enough apart for a moment of sanity to creep in and derail things before it got out of hand.

If they wanted to step back from that precipice.

Carlota found that she really didn't want to. Erika smiled and it warmed a spot inside Carlota that had been cold so long that she thought it was supposed to be like that. Except that it had started to melt.

She found her shoulders coming down. They'd been relaxed, but now a certain tension seemed to bleed out of them as they just sat and stared at each other.

"I've been sitting here, trying to decide if I really wanted to do this," Erika said quietly. "This is out of character for me, but feels right. Feels good, even. You?"

Carlota rolled up onto her knees on the couch so she could lean forward, over Erika's upturned face, and kiss her. That felt good. A hand came up and touched her face, caressing her cheek before trailing down to her neck.

Carlota put a hand down to hold her weight and let Erika pull her deeper into the kiss. Inside, she felt that cold spot melt some more.

How long had it been since she'd been with a woman who might know what she was doing? Decades, it seemed.

Most agents were men. Ergo, you sent a woman to seduce them. Conversely, most civilians in the places you wanted to penetrate tended to be female, and then, men were called for.

Rarely did a woman agent get a chance to enjoy herself in the field with another woman. And Carlota hadn't had a fling like this, not counting Armand, in... *We will not discuss that number aloud, lest we tempt the gods to do something rude.*

She kissed the woman.

They ended up stretched out on the couch, pressed full-length against each other. Clothing got loosened.

Carlota had worn an A-line dress tonight. Cut like a sundress, but in a much heavier cloth. Her belt took a little work, the two of them not willing to stand up to remove it.

Finally, Erika got it loose and coiled it like a sleepy snake on the floor next to two pairs of shoes. Erika's vest covered it a few moments later, along with her shirt.

Carlota felt a fever take hold of her where that span of ice had been at the start of the evening. She got Erika nude, then rolled off the couch to stand before the woman's adoring eyes and pull her dress up over her head.

Neither of them had tan lines. Carlota had been expecting something, but found that the woman was such a perfect match that she wondered if someone had managed to read her mind and place the perfect trap in front of her.

Perfect.

They returned to the couch, arms around each other. Legs curling as well. Hands exploring. Mouths exploring.

Time passed. Carlota lost track of anything except touch on her skin and the salty taste where she kissed Erika.

The bog troll had been wonderful. Erika seemed to instinctively understand where that man had set a bar, and was assiduously working to clear it.

Carlota almost whimpered when Erika suddenly sat back and got up, standing over her like a sex goddess offering three wishes. One set of hands remained clenched together.

"If I don't do it now, I will forget and miss my appointment to get my hair done in the morning," Erika said in a husky, emotional voice, standing there, her nude perfection almost taunting Carlota's need. "Don't go anywhere."

Carlota nodded and watched the play of muscles in the woman's back and bottom as she crossed the room to the desk and picked up the handset, glancing back over her shoulder with a mischievous grin as she wiggled her butt.

Carlota considered joining the woman over there. Sneaking up behind her so she could wrap hands around that waist. Pull those hips back. Reach up and cup her breasts while nibbling on her shoulder.

"This is room five-four-oh-six," Erika said, trying to sound utterly normal. "I'd like a wakeup call for six AM, please. Thank you."

She hung up before Carlota could make up her mind to

go over there and maul the woman, then turned and looked back at her, eyes glittering.

"I changed my mind," Erika said. "The bed will be much more comfortable than the couch."

She took two steps this direction and held out a hand in invitation.

Carlota rose and walked right into the woman, pressing herself hungrily against the warm flesh and considering what lucky thing had happened to her tonight.

After everything that had happened to her, didn't she deserve a little pleasure in her life?

Outside this room, the game was getting hot and heavy.

Carlota and Erika could match it.

16

ALICIA HUNG UP THE HANDSET AND TRIED TO PROCESSES the words. That had been Mac's voice. And Mac's room. But she'd been pretending to be talking to the front desk.

Ergo, she wasn't alone.

At the same time, she hadn't said any of the key words they'd set up in case someone got captured or arrested, so she didn't seem to be in trouble.

Alicia checked the clock. She'd been deep inside a local database maintained by one of the criminal syndicates on *Borlait*. Junior varsity people, but still criminals. They had more interesting contacts than most of the cops did around here.

Still, Mac was up to something. Alicia sighed and backed out of that system. She was pretty sure she could get back in later. The fools they'd hired to set up their systems had left default passwords all over the place, so the first thing Alicia had done had been to give herself super-administrator privileges.

They'd need to pretty much wipe the system bare to the metal to block her out next time.

Instead, Alicia turned on the room's vidscreen and tuned it to cameras she'd set in Mac's room when they arrived.

Oh, wow. Mac had herself a date. Cute brunette with dark skin and a rangy build.

Alicia found herself a little turned on, watching the two nude women neck before turning and heading to the bedroom. She switched cameras and played voyeur as Mac turned down the comforter and sheets, then invited the woman to join her.

Except that Mac wouldn't have called like that if she just got lucky. Well, maybe, but she'd been acting like this was normal, so something must be up.

Otherwise, she'd have said she had company and not to knock too early. So the stranger wasn't supposed to know that Mac wasn't alone.

Alicia zoomed the camera and panned it a little to get a good view of the woman. Mac must have been setting the stranger up, because she'd laid down in such a way as to not obscure anything, and they were nude atop the sheets as they necked.

Alicia started snapping pictures. Full body as well as face. At one point, the woman turned almost perfectly face-on to the camera as Mac did something. The look was particularly good, very polite, almost a tiny orgasm. Still, it let her get bones scanned cleanly.

She tuned out the performance and focused on her computer, trying not to get turned on and glad she'd left the sound off from what looked like moans of pleasure on faces.

Female. Middle-aged. Hispanic skin tones, with matching hair and dark eyes. Darker than most of *Salonnia*, but not that much. Better fit in *Aquitaine*, or all along the long border the two shared.

And Mac wanted Alicia to know about the woman. Who was she?

She grabbed her comm and pinged Handsome.

"What's up?" he answered almost immediately. It was late and he'd said he was staying in tonight, after several nights of breaking and entering in various places that had all largely been dead ends, but he was obviously awake.

"Mac has company in her room," Alicia said. "She just called here like I was the front desk and asked for a wakeup call tomorrow at six."

"Set your alarm and be sure to call," Rob said tersely. "And sound like the front desk when you do."

"Okay?"

"You watching right now?" he continued.

"Sort of," Alicia admitted. "Mac brought a woman home and they're rather enjoying themselves in the bedroom as I talk to you."

"No alarms?" he asked.

"None beyond that phone call."

"I'll be right up to see you," he said. "Something doesn't smell right."

Alicia hung up and had to agree. The women were having fun, but why call?

Unless Mac thought that she'd stumbled into one of those enemy agents? Handsome had already gotten more than two dozen folks to walk in front of cameras Alicia owned. They only got positive matches from her records on about ten, so the mission was a huge success on those grounds alone.

Alicia checked her supply of snacks and drinks. She might be suddenly stuck in the room doing surveillance things and didn't want to get room service too many times in a row. She could always send Handsome for take-out, if the mission had just turned inside out and Mac had someone on the hook.

It was only fair, after all.

He knocked on the door quickly. Alicia confirmed that it was him then opened the bolts to let the man in.

He was wearing a nice cologne tonight. Foresty. He always smelled good.

They ended up on the couch that she'd commandeered as a command post, watching the big screen across from them as Mac and another woman…*did things to each other*.

Alicia found herself getting a little flustered, watching that while she was smelling him next to her.

"Do we know anything?" he asked, turning to look at her.

Luckily, Handsome was at the other end of the couch. Far enough away. Probably.

"Nothing," Alicia replied. "She doesn't show up in my records, but that doesn't mean anything, since I've left our local teams alone. They might know who she was, but they might not."

He nodded, pensive, then turned back.

Alicia stole sidelong glances at the man, even as she watched the women.

Mac and her friend were oblivious. Someone might blow the door to the suite off the hinges and not get their attention.

Alicia was willing to admit that she was jealous. Like, hungry jealous. That was hot. She was getting uncomfortable, watching it with Handsome and his forest smell carbonating her hormones harder and harder.

"Longshot," he muttered under his breath.

"What is?"

"Female," he pointed at the screen. "I'd guess her to be mid-to-late forties, but I could be a six years off either direction. Mac's definitely not an exhibitionist, so this isn't just her rubbing our faces in her getting lucky tonight with a hot babe."

"Babe?" Alicia asked. "She's not that much. I realize I'm not one to talk, but that one's only cute. Not anywhere near as hot as Mac. Curvy, but not particularly busty or slinky. Just kinda woman, middle-aged like you said and in good shape."

She realized that he'd gone perfectly still. Maybe not even breathing.

"You have a face capture of her?" he said without turning this way.

"Sure." Alicia started typing and brought up several different stills she had extracted from the video. "What are we looking for?"

"Field agents need to be bland," he spoke quietly. "Mildly attractive, because homely is memorable, as is beautiful. The Service uses me as a blunt instrument or a scalpel these days, rather than an operative, because I tend to stand out. I draw missions where that's useful. Same with Mac. She sucks all the oxygen out of any room she's in, which lets me vanish into the background like we did last year. The woman with Mac looks more like the sort of field agent most places recruit. I wonder if she's one of us."

It didn't help that he had all that, AND brains. Alicia could be jealous of him, too. He wasn't as smart as her or Mac, but he also didn't try to prove that he was. Instead, he assumed that she was smarter and better at her thing than everybody else, and took advantage of that.

If only she could get him to take advantage of *her*.

"What was that?" he asked, glancing back her direction.

Alicia realized she'd been muttering and slammed her mouth shut.

Rob turned to face her.

"You okay?" he asked.

Alicia gestured to the screen.

"Flustered, watching that performance," she admitted. "Turned on and a little horny. No, that is not an invitation."

He'd opened his mouth to say something, but paused, studying her.

"What I was about to say was that I wasn't inviting myself," Handsome turned serious on her. "But if you need, I am available. And safe. You can't always assure that in the field. Truth be told, I'm kinda wound up watching this, and I know Mac in that way."

"So if I needed you to take me off-line at some point…?" Alicia began hesitantly.

She wasn't sure what she'd need, but Mac had whispered a few things. And the man had a reputation in the building as a protege of Jorge Royo.

Maybe she needed to avail herself of the opportunity?

"I'd be happy to help," Handsome smiled. "Now, or should I go back down to my room before we get a little overwhelmed here?"

She considered it. *REALLY* considered it.

But that was an open invitation she could claim some other time, when she wasn't so horny her eyes wanted to cross.

Plus, she had the face of a total stranger that needed to be filtered through every dataset she could penetrate.

Bad choice of words. As was seduce into giving up their secrets.

"Another time," Alicia managed, in spite of what certain parts of her anatomy might have wanted. "Gonna stay up late and do some homework on the stranger."

He nodded and rose. The man seemed to be breathing a little heavy.

Like maybe he wanted her? She'd never dated much beyond the nerds in school, but Alicia had known herself to be too squishy and way too wrapped up in her mental and intellectual superiority.

Having a guy like Handsome Rob looking at her with lust in his eyes was almost overwhelming, especially on top of things happening on the screen.

Thank the creator she had the sound off, even if she was recording everything for later.

Not that she'd watch it later in privacy. Heaven forbid.

"Remember to set your alarm," Handsome said as he moved to the door and let himself out without looking back.

That was good. She might have called him back *to take care of things* otherwise. Since everything was recording, she fed the face pics into an algorithm she'd written and started it brute-forcing for matches in the background.

That would take a while. She dutifully set an alarm for five-thirty, so she was ready for whatever happened in the morning.

She really needed a cold shower about now.

17

Rob had gotten up at five. Showered, shaved, dressed for field work. The weather was a bit blustery this morning from a front that had blown in, so heavy pants and a light rain shell in blue. His hair was a little longer than normal for *Borlait*, but that was mostly just the resorts demanding high and tight on the men and something equally disruptive on the women.

He looked more like a tourist. Dressed like it. It would make him stand out a little, but only against the background of people who were normally invisible and wanting to be left alone on their day off.

Sun would rise soon, but not that soon. Hopefully, Mac and the strange women had planned on getting up at six, then showering. Or fooling around before showering.

He made his way across the street and chose a spot with a view of the main hotel entrance out the window of a twenty-four-hour dive restaurant. Borlait days ran twenty-one standard hours, with local hours themselves sliced so that there were twenty-four of them in a day.

Sun would rise before seven, but he wanted to be in a position to handle things.

Helped that he had the front of the restaurant mostly to himself, with a few singles up at a bar facing the kitchen. Food wasn't all that great, but it was difficult to fuck up sausage and eggs in the first place, and he was just here to be out of sight when watching.

There was no way to tell what the stranger would do in the morning. She and Mac might lay in bed all morning and then finally make their way downstairs for brunch.

Rob had to presume that the cover of a wakeup call was to ensure that the stranger left at a reasonable time. And that he and Alicia could follow her.

If she just got a taxi, Alicia would probably be able to hack into their systems before it had taken off. Security on those sorts of things just wasn't prepared for the kinds of horsepower that a government-level spy service could bring to bear, which was why he'd brought her.

Rob was across the street in case the stranger decided to walk somewhere. Hopefully, not across the street to grab a bite as Rob would be trapped in the act of leaving and have to send Alicia.

He checked his watch. Ten minutes to six. Alicia should be awake.

He sent her a message.

* *Just in case, you be dressed and ready for tailing someone shortly – R* *

That way, he could simply walk right by the stranger if she did go for dive food, and Alicia could get involved. Not the best solution, but he didn't have any other resources.

His comm beeped.

* *Understood. – A* *

And she was awake so she could give Mac the wakeup call requested.

He sat back with his coffee as the waiter picked up the last of his food. He pretended to read the news as six o'clock came and went, uncertain as to what would happen next.

* *Wakeup call delivered. They are not in a hurry to get gone. – A* *

Rob suppressed a snort. Alicia had been extremely hot and bothered last night, watching the two women. He had as well, but that was normal. And he might always find an excuse to do things like that for Mac one of these days.

Or to her. Whatever.

He presumed they had stirred, maybe gone and peed, and then climbed back into a warm bed to fool around some more this morning from Alicia's note.

He got more coffee and remained engrossed in his news, looking up every once in a while and looking around, like he was expecting someone that hadn't called to let him know they had overslept.

Something.

Do nothing to stand out while on surveillance. Fit into the framework of the setting and be another character.

He'd been taking acting classes at a local community college in Puerto Peñasco, back on *Ramsey*. Most of his fellow students were either a decade older or a decade younger, heavily tilted towards the female such that he got pulled into any scene that needed a male speaker.

Jorge had suggested it. Rob was going to ask Miguel for permission to audition for some commercials and such at some point, just because then he might be unconsciously seen as *that guy* when folks noticed him, and he could talk about being an actor.

Much better than a spy. Or a professional killer.

The classes were giving him a different view of things than Service training. It let him be part of the scene that might suddenly step up and have a speaking part, instead of vanishing entirely into the background, which is what you expected out of your field agents.

*Okay, finally showering. – A *

Rob snorted and ordered a side of sausage for the extra protein. He explained to the waiter that he thought his breakfast date had forgotten to set an alarm, but that he was going to wait a bit longer before he gave up.

The man commiserated and refilled Rob's coffee.

Rob was looking forward to debriefing Mac, if only to torture her by walking her through the complete seduction, in all its gory details. Probably make Alicia record it, just to torture her, too.

At least he'd be able to nail down an enemy agent, because Rob was pretty sure he was looking at one of the big players.

Not Emil Yankov, from Imperial Intelligence, but someone at that level of the game. Someone Miguel would want to know, if only so that he could put her picture in front of everyone everywhere and utterly blow her cover.

That, or turn her and have a double-agent inside somebody's shop. If she'd spent the night with Mac and then fooled around this morning before taking a joint shower, there was a vulnerability somebody could exploit, more likely than not.

Mac might be running her own agents in the field soon. Hell of a cover.

*Goodbye kiss occurring. – A *

Rob wolfed down the sausages and rose to pay, obviously surrendering in the fight but not calling someone to rag on them about standing him up.

He moved slowly, deliberately, just so he could emerge from the restaurant at roughly the same time as the target. Alicia would have said something if the woman suddenly summoned a cab, so he had to presume that she was going to walk at least some distance before doing so.

Or walking right by him to get some eggs. Something.

He had her picture memorized. Cute, as Alicia had said, but not stunning in the manner of Mac. Average in a lot of ways, which fit his usual description of agents.

You wanted them non-memorable physically, while recruiting the smartest ones you could find. He knew he was bright, but that was mostly street hustler smarts. Mac and Alicia were advanced mathematics-professors smart.

He would assume an enemy agent who was at least as smart and trained as he was, until proven otherwise. In fact, the better she turned out to be, the more he could assign her a role in this weird drama.

There.

Rob watched her emerge from the big double slider doors alone and step out front. Two men up front who handled newly arrived or departing guests spoke with her briefly, but she waved them off cheerfully, at least from what he could see, and started walking on foot.

Rob stayed just inside the door of the restaurant, counted her steps, and emerged once she had committed to a direction.

He was across the street from the stranger, but she was dressed too nicely to blend in with the exercise weirdos around, or the early business folk. She didn't seem to be paying that much attention, but he wasn't about to let down his guard.

They were headed deeper in towards downtown, which suited him fine. If she lived around here, he could find the building and have Alicia do things to track her. If she got a cab, he had a delivery address.

Rob pulled in all his antennae and pretended to be just

another slob out too late and staggering home, much like the woman ahead and across.

He was hunting.

18

CARLOTA KISSED ERIKA GOODBYE WITH A SERIOUS twinge of regret. It was everything she could do not to stay for a while and get emotionally involved with her. Bog troll had been fantastic. Erika had cleared that bar with so much to spare that she might have set it to a new level.

It would be a hard act to follow.

Still, she made it downstairs and caught that first hint of morning chill. The temperature had dropped a bit from yesterday and the streets were slick.

Carlota considered calling a cab, but wanted to walk.

She needed to process things, and did that better in motion than she could sitting in her room and meditating.

Or fermenting. Whatever it was she did there.

Armand had touched things in her mind she'd mostly forgotten about. Erika had dusted off cold spots and warmed them.

What was she doing right now? Playing a deadly game with *Salonnian* and other intelligence agencies. Tweaking their noses that she was better than they had given her credit for. Better than them, if she pulled it off.

Then what?

Up until now, Carlota realized that she'd been hoping they would come to their senses and offer her back her old job as a field agent. In the cold, damp, chill of morning, proudly slut-walking her way home, she understood that the Bureau wasn't going to thank her.

They were going to bury her. Every day that passed, they would get angrier with her, especially when everyone got to Chapter Seven and she started talking about folks who were still working. Politicians who were still in the limelight trying to win elections, or at least influence things. Agents out in the field who might not be known to the general public, but would be to other agencies.

The kinds of dirty dealing that would compromise a lot of folks.

Make them extra angry.

And what was she going to get out of it? Fame? Some. That just made her a bigger target.

Money? She had a stupendous amount stashed away. And the ability to score more from a variety of things if it got tight. With Armand's help, she'd made enough to live quite comfortably for at least a year, just in one night.

And what had it gotten her?

Hiding in a hotel. Sneaking out in disguise and seducing complete strangers. Or letting them seduce her. Armand and Erika had both been wild cards in her planning that just showed Carlota how much the rest of her life had gotten bland and almost banal.

She wasn't living. She was marking time.

Until what?

Until when?

What was her endgame?

She came to almost a violent stop as it dawned on her. They were going to kill her.

Worse, she'd set the rules of the game such that she'd drawn all the hunters to *Borlait* so she could thwart them personally. There was no way off this planet, she was guessing, short of somehow smuggling herself out. Or stealing a ship and surviving making a run for it.

Did she kidnap some woman cop who was trying to watch the starport and use her credentials to escape, pretending to be the other woman long enough to get gone?

She didn't want to die.

And looking back, that had been the implicit outcome. She'd gone into this with rage and it had gotten her here. Trapped her.

Death wish. Make them kill her because they couldn't stand that she was better than they were.

Passively suicidal. Death by cop, or death by agent. Same difference. Because she didn't have anything else she could do but be a spy.

Did she?

She had been trained as a card sharp by a man who understood that a pretty woman at the table altered the equations at what was frequently an all-male endeavor.

Carlota certainly didn't want to find some sugar daddy to take care of her. Worse, none would, because she'd be competing with perky, little bimbos half her age, willing to do *anything* for that brass ring.

Which was exactly why some men chased them, because women like her didn't have any fucks left to give at their behavior, so they had to find someone dumb enough, green enough, *desperate enough*, to put up with them.

Creator willing, Carlota would never be that put upon.

Which left strangers and random couplings. Was that all she wanted out of life?

No.

Worse, she didn't want to die right now by her own

stupidity, and had no good idea how to slip out of the trap that she had created for herself.

Carlota wasn't even sure that she could escape, or if the rules of the game would demand her head on a stake in order to complete everything.

She'd made a monumental error at the beginning. Baked it into the project, because her subconscious mind had been preparing to die, and wanting to go out in a blaze of glory.

And she suddenly didn't want to die.

Carlota physically shook herself, feeling almost like a wet dog as she emerged from whatever terrible place she'd walked herself into. She looked around, but the streets were much thinner with foot traffic than they would be later in the day, when the sun came up.

A few joggers. A few folks going in to work. A few, like her, stumbling home from a too-late night that had hopefully turned out as fantastically awesome as hers had.

Or at least close enough.

Carlota pulled out her comm and opened it with shaky fingers.

She wanted to live, and was surrounded on all sides by angry folks who had nothing to lose by chasing her with ever-escalating firepower and deniability.

Worse, she was truly outlaw now, with all that entailed.

She called a cab, because she needed to get someplace quiet to think.

There had to be a way out of this.

Right?

19

ROB STUDIED PEOPLE. JORGE HAD KNOWN HOW THE Service trained couriers and agents, and generally approved, but he'd also had some choice observations over and above that. Seasoning the pan, as he had called it one night when they were both alone and a little drunk.

Good, cast iron skillets should never be fully cleaned. You left some of the old grease in place to flavor things, layering them over the years like sedimentary rock.

Most agents were bright, clean pans, polished nicely, with nothing stuck to them. To a man like Jorge Royo, they stood out because normal humans didn't ever look like that. Most agents and agencies never saw that, though. They saw other agents, all alike.

All standing out.

So Jorge had suggested a small library of books, a couple of classes, and several weird, late-night-high-end cable channel movies—a few of them his—each of which had been found to contain some really interesting observations about human nature.

Rob had been walking liesurely, sliding seamlessly in and

out of the slowly-building morning foot traffic. Not a lot of people, but enough to hide him from his target. Enough that he wasn't really visible to his target. This was a job where agents tailing someone might show up as anomalies to an aware person.

She came to a stop so suddenly he was certain he'd been made, except that she seemed to be staring at the horizon. Rob found a nearby donut shop and considered slipping in to buy himself one, but that might take too long if she'd spooked. He wanted to keep her in sight, so he watched her out of the corner of his eye in the glass front over the cases as though arguing with himself about diet or something.

Seasoning the pan. That woman appeared to be having a sudden crisis. Emotional, most likely. Moral, maybe, but there weren't any morals in this game. Hardly any ethics other than to protect your side, regardless of what you thought of them individually, while doing dirty to the other side, no matter how polite and friendly they might be when you weren't on an opposing operation.

No, she was suddenly staring at metaphorical oncoming traffic as she stood paralyzed in the crosswalk of the universe, about to be a bug on a windshield.

Or something like that.

Rob watched the woman almost literally walk herself through the clinical stages of death. Eerie. He did that occasionally, but only late at night, in the privacy of his secured flat and his mind.

Never on a street corner in front of God and everybody.

She shimmied. Turned around to look at everyone, without once alighting on him.

Rob watched her reach for a comm in her pocket ,so he stepped to the door of the donut shop, pulling the door open as the woman did something.

He pulled out his own comm and dialed. Now was not a

good place or time to do this, because there was always a chance he would blow his cover if another agent had gotten the munchies this morning.

At the same time, he didn't have much choice.

Alicia answered instantly.

"Yes?"

"Down six blocks, at the corner of Madison and Fourteenth," he said quietly. "She might be summoning a ride. I need you to track her from this moment if she is."

"You certain about the cab?" Alicia asked.

"Gut instinct," Rob replied.

Looking out the window, the woman was standing there holding her comm like a divining rod seeking water.

Or salvation.

"Okay, I have a request call from that location for one rider," Alicia said. "Now what?"

"She's yours," he said. "I'm out of the game, so I'll grab some donuts and walk back in a few minutes. Make sure Mac is awake and down with you when I get there."

He hung up and got into line with a few other bleary-eyed folks. A dozen of various things would be nice, though he'd already eaten.

Something strange had just happened and he didn't know what.

It did not fit the pattern of a field agent doing field agent things, but he needed to talk to Mac to understand what had happened last night. And this morning.

Something wasn't right.

20

ALICIA HAD BROKEN HERSELF INTO THE PUBLIC transport network early on. Lots of folks didn't own private vehicles on this planet so they rode the subways out to resorts or around one of several rings. Or they called taxis for short-term things when they could afford it. Tourists and locals with money for the most part.

Mac's date had triggered a call. Alicia might have noticed it just looking around, but Handsome nailed it right down, so she watched as a driver was dispatched, drove up, and got himself a customer. Individual cars were too difficult to access, but the overall system involved a lot of unencrypted chatter going back and forth.

Quickly, Alicia had the destination, as well as the name of the credit account that was paying. She pinged Mac as she watched the screen.

"Good morning," Mac said. "What's our status?"

"Handsome was tracking her, but she just called a cab," Alicia replied. "He's headed back here and bringing donuts. Asked me to ask you to be here because I'm watching her now."

"Be down in five," Mac said, cutting the line and leaving Alicia alone with her technological toys and her thoughts.

She focused on tracing the cab as it wended its way into one of those weird, little cluster neighborhoods where an older, upper-middle-class space had somehow remained intact, even as blue collar filled in seven-eighths around it. Probably a place with political connections, back in the day.

One older convention center, anchoring a neighborhood that might have been an outer suburb at one point, before Bennan reached out and swallowed it. Several restaurants. A couple of museums. Bunch of separate houses with old yards instead of towers of flats.

Mac arrived first, freshly everythinged and lovely. Getting laid like that would put a smile on anybody's face in the morning.

Handsome showed up about the time that a Bevel Harri, at least that was the name on her credit accounts, got dropped off at one of five hotels in her destination neighborhood. Alicia didn't own any of the security cameras in the vicinity, so she couldn't be sure that the woman actually walked in, but it gave her a starting point.

"What do we know?" Handsome asked.

He'd brought a box of fresh donuts and a carafe of coffee, so Alicia would be willing to forgive him for almost any sins today.

"She went directly to a hotel from here, out in Harnaby," Alicia said. "Name given as Bevel Harri. Haven't had much time to track her down past that, but we have an opening."

Both of them turned to Mac. Alicia watched the woman blush profusely for a moment before drawing a deep breath.

"She one of us?" Handsome began.

"That was the feeling I got off her last night," Mac said. "A falseness that felt like another agent. At the time I wondered if somebody like you had been smart enough to bring someone like me along to get inside Carlota's mind."

"But?" Handsome asked.

"But she reacted wrong that way as well," Mac said.

"How so?" Alicia interjected. "You two seemed quite copacetic."

Oh, wow, *that* was a blush and three-quarters.

"She seemed to really react to me, but I've been so deep inside Carlota's mind that I'm not sure she wasn't picking up on all that hunger and need," Mac finally sputtered. Then her voice almost down to a whisper. "What if that was Carlota?"

Everything went quiet. Both of them stared at Mac. Alicia wondered if the look on her face mirrored the horror that Rob seemed to be experiencing.

"What?" somebody asked.

"I've been trying to identify her by identifying *with* her," Mac said carefully. "Getting inside that particular rage of a woman who's been wronged and cast aside in favor of younger, smarter, prettier. Something-er. We're about the same age. The same in a lot of ways. She specifically struck me as having all of the physical and social characteristics we look for in field agents as you've described it to me. How many other fifty-year-old female field agents do you suppose there are?"

"Could she be a stringer for some Syndicate?" Alicia asked, trying to make sure they didn't go down the wrong rabbit hole. "As you said, maybe someone else wanted to figure out how Carlota would think, so they brought their own version."

"Either way, we need to know who she is," Handsome stated. "If she's somebody's agent, we need to know who."

"What if that was Carlota?" Alicia asked.

"Then we better hope that we didn't spook her,"

Handsome said. "Because until we have somebody better to work with, that's our best lead yet and I intend to follow it."

"Do we know who else is in play?" Mac asked. "Without assuming anything about Helen? Or Bevel? Or whoever she ends up being. Just the fact that she called herself Helen last night doesn't condemn her. Maybe she has a husband and that was just a fling?"

"Go out to a show by yourself?" Handsome almost sneered. "Pick up a stranger and go home with them? Did she call and let anybody know not to wait up for her?"

"She did not," Mac nodded. "And she was hungry for touch. Ravenous, almost. So she wasn't getting what she needed at home."

"Good enough," Handsome declared. "Alicia, you find out everything you can about the woman. I am willing to bet that there's hardly anything there when you start looking, but now we know why, since she's not a real human anyway. Then start looking to see if she meets up with others that we can trace outwards and build up some sort of network diagram of whatever agency she represents."

"And if she has no agency?" Alicia asked.

"Then she might be Carlota Rojas," he said simply. "In which case we have to figure out what to do with her."

"What do you mean?"

"She's a *Salonnian* agent, Alicia," he reminded her. "They are going to be after her. Emil Yankov is after her. A lot of people want her. One of them might spook her. Or they might kill her."

"What about us?"

She didn't like the way he held up a hand, palm up. Too much unknown.

That meant anything might happen.

"What about that Imperial?" Mac asked. "Yankov?"

"He's next on my list," Handsome said.

Alicia couldn't help the shudder that passed through her body at the deadly look on his face.

21

Emil had just completed the latest visit to Constanz's office. At least the man was willing to play along, once Emil had offered to cover his expenses. A pittance, in the scheme of things, but paying the salary for an extra body to copy and organize the chapters as they came in, preparing the book for publication, probably meant the difference between profit and loss for the publishing house.

If nothing else, it gave them somebody who could file and organize things the rest of the week. Goodness knew Constanz needed that, too.

Now Emil was heading back to his hotel, a three-ring binder stashed in a messenger-style bag he'd acquired for this. He felt a little silly. Far too old to be mistaken for such a person as a courier, but perhaps he was a lawyer transporting important papers between offices as part of a deal being signed.

Something.

Always be in character in public. Always have a motivation, a style of speech, a walk that is different from others.

Never be you, although after this many decades Emil wasn't entirely sure who this Yankov fellow might be.

It would not be something he discovered in retirement, either. The layers had been painted on so thick over the decades that he was reasonably certain that the wood underneath had rotted away at some point, leaving only the paint itself.

All good agents ended up like that.

He would wear this same, short-brimmed cap that made him look like a fishing captain, though. Emil discovered that he liked it. It spoke to him.

More importantly, it spoke *of him*.

That was a starting point for whoever he might be next. Some retired grandpa having a day off from spoiling the younglings. Perhaps headed to get coffee with old friends and tell lies about how good things used to be before the kids these days.

That Emil had no friends was immaterial. He had always had a knack for instantly making old friends. For cultivating strangers in such a way that they joined you for dinner and were telling the really good dirty jokes they knew in only a few minutes.

It was a talent he'd had early, and made the most of over his decades as a spy.

Coffee sounded good right now, for reasons he was old enough to admit had nothing to do with any operation. Just sitting in a public space and people watching. Making up stories about utter strangers. In his old days, that had been a training element.

Sit in public with your handler and identify folks by temperament and personality, from the way they dressed. The order they drank. The way they parted their hair, even.

Yes, coffee. Nobody around him would understand the

immense magnitude of the words in front of him as he read the latest installment.

Truth be told, most wouldn't care. Governments were expected to do these things to one another, and rarely did it matter in the overall scheme of things.

Emil caught himself short of squirreling in down that particular train of thought and found a donut shop that was still open. Possibly transitioning to just coffee at this point.

He made his way inside and noted the crowd. A few young mothers or fathers with offspring, out for a bit of early afternoon sunlight. Two businessmen and a woman who looked to be their boss, huddled around a table furtively muttering about something that was none of his business, once he made sure that they weren't competitors.

There is a way a person walks that makes most of them stand out. Identifying it had taken a lot of training for Emil. Breaking his own underlings of it took time.

Some washed out over it.

He found himself fourth in line, musing about four decades in the industry and how *Hummingbird* had gotten herself here. Of course a woman that old had little to offer in the field. Only a small subset of folks ever looked at a woman like that and knew lust. Better to dangle young ones in front of them, the kind that had been carefully selected to look pretty and act dumb.

Men could easily be led astray that way.

Emil shook his head and let the smell of hot grease just bathe him in sweetness. They were close to out of almost everything, but as long as nobody in front of him ordered two dozen, he could treat himself to something.

Hummingbird had run far longer than anybody back on *St. Legier* or *Salonnia* proper had expected. Anybody but Emil, anyway. Upping her own game felt like a last-ditch desperation as the hounds closed in.

She had been lucky enough so far, but her luck was due to run out soon.

As he reached the front of the line, everyone else had gotten one donut, so he had options.

He marked it down to the excellence of his own luck and concentrated on his choices.

Sit in a spot with a view of the sidewalk, sip some coffee, munch a pastry, and read up on the latest outrages that woman sought to perpetrate on an innocent galaxy.

She didn't have long.

22

Rob had marked the man when he emerged from the building, looking innocent and harmless.

Emil Yankov himself. A name hundreds of times more famous than his nearly unknown face. Almost Jorge's exact opposite in that way, since nobody new Jorge Royo was an agent.

Notes in Constanz's office had indicated that he had a full process in place now for the Imperial agent when a new chapter arrived. Make eleven copies instead of the ten they used to. Constanz couldn't trust a temp, but he'd hired one to free up space for his own staff, so they printed out a copy for Yankov, three-hole punched it for the man's binder that he would bring, and then contacted him to pick it up.

Rob grinned at the foolishness of any agent having a pattern so predictable. Apparently, it had never dawned on the Grand Old Man of Imperial Intelligence that he might be prey, here on *Borlait*.

Someone that old had to be close to retirement from Imperial Intelligence. And he was nobody Rob would have known on a sidewalk, but that wasn't important. He'd gotten some fantastic pictures of the man, with his carefully trimmed white beard and cute hat. One of them had been a telephoto where Yankov had almost seemed to be staring into the lens, except that his eyes were elsewhere.

Everyone would have excellent images with which to identify the man, although there was a chance that this was some other agent who fit Yankov's profile and was using his name in public; but Rob felt like this was really the old ghost of *St. Legier* himself, finally in daylight.

Either way, Miguel would either know the fellow, or be able to flood his picture everywhere and utterly blow him for future undercover operations.

Not that this fellow was being particularly undercover here. Nope, right out in the open. Not a care in the world. That fit stories Rob had heard about Yankov. Biggest elephant in the area, stomping right down the middle of the trail because nobody hunted monsters that big.

Except that everybody was food for somebody. Jorge had reinforced that lesson many times. Legends spoke of a tribe of tiny folk, back in the prehistoric era on Earth, who dug their pits right in the middle of a game trail and covered it over with grass and leaves, for somebody so big to walk along and fall in, at which point it either broke its neck, or snapped a leg and was trapped.

They'd sit above and pelt it with spears, then eat it when it finally died.

And even the ones that died of old age eventually got eaten by ants.

Nobody escapes.

So Rob watched an enemy agent of unknown provenance that might be the top agent in *Fribourg* walk into a coffee and donut shop like a man without a care in the world. From across the street and down a bit, Rob had a lucky view as Yankov got himself into line with locals.

Yesterday, Rob had found a similar sort of place while tracking the agent they were still calling Helen for now, pending positive identification as Carlota. Rob's gut told him that it was her.

Weird and random luck, but in this game you manufactured your fortune. He'd brought Mac, and told her to indulge in the fantasies of rage and recrimination that Carlota had spoken about in her introduction and first chapter. That both women might have ended up close enough together to seduce each other just meant that she'd pulled it off, a stunning coup that she could use on whoever replaced Miguel when he finally retired.

Keep her in the field. Carlota Rojas had shown that she was still good. And lucky. Mac was the same, and probably smarter and more dangerous, if she chose to go out in a similar blaze of glory.

Except that Mac was appreciated, both for her brains as well as her body. He owed Jorge a bottle of thirty-year scotch at some point for boxing his ears about noticing how sexy a woman could be after thirty, let alone forty.

Roxy liked to occasionally play the sexpot, just because so many people had their own fantasies about the elusive Mrs. Jones, once the most beautiful woman in the galaxy and still in anybody's top ten, having retired from the action roles that required an expert stunt double to become even more of a thespian. And win more awards.

Age was an enemy you could never beat. Only hold at bay for a time. But even then it snuck up and bit you when you weren't looking. He'd be thirty soon, and most folks approached that number with some sort of *finally-growing-up* mental reset. Mac was over fifty, and still turned heads when she wanted to.

And when she didn't. He'd seen her bleary-eyed wuth bed-head, first thing in the morning.

Still a completely lustworthy babe.

Rob put away his camera, stashing it in a pocket. He'd settled on an electronic one today, rather than bringing long glass. These pics didn't need to be museum quality. Just enough to nail somebody. And Emil Yankov really had been the one who walked out of that office. He was as nailed as Rob could get.

One of the legends in this game. Jorge Royo, if the actor had taken the first offer and gone inside the Service, rather than maintaining a complete side lifestyle as an agent while making movies, playing golf, and competing in tanning competitions.

Rob decided that he wanted to see what kind of a man Yankov was up close, this Imperial Intelligence hotshot. Someone they'd sent from *St. Legier* itself, to participate in the chase, if not one of the coordinators.

Rob didn't have a team, beyond those two, dangerous women. He'd stack them up against whoever *Fribourg* had dispatched. Or the locals who were almost blunderingly bad.

He'd wondered at first why she had chosen *Borlait* as the spot for her game. There were better places to hide. Planets with a billion souls to slide sideways into.

After a month here, he understood. *Salonnia* was run by the Syndicates, ancient oligarchies that had turned themselves into criminal organizations by keeping a thumb on the cops and politicians. If you could get your own folks out of trouble for smuggling and such, while making everyone else pay, you came out ahead.

Salonnia had never impressed him. *Borlait* was run by competing teams of criminals, each backing a different one of the major or minor resorts like pearls on a string around Bennan. They didn't want laws enforced. So you had a planetary government that was largely absent, and geared towards protecting tourists and employees from predators, because you needed both to have a successful economy.

Past that, just about anything went, and the undercover agents and cops Rob had seen locally were a joke.

Except Emil Yankov himself was apparently here, so *Fribourg* had understood that they would need serious firepower. And sent it.

He didn't want to bump the man, but Rob found that he wanted to know the fellow closer. Or at closer range, which was the same thing.

Crossing the street, he made his way to the front of the coffee shop for a donut.

23

ROB DEARLY LOVED THE SMELL OF HOT GREASE AND sugar. So much so that he had to limit himself, because he knew that his metabolism would slow down again soon. Better to be in the habit of not indulging, so he didn't have to spend so much extra time in the pool or the gym working it off.

Today was an exception. An indulgence.

He wasn't trying to track the man any more than he had this far. It would have taken a dedicated team of agents undercover to follow somebody like Yankov through the crowded sidewalks of Bennan without being made.

Rob just wanted to see who the man was when he wasn't on stage.

Everyone was always on stage in this business. Only Jorge had managed to turn it into an art form while being paid for it.

Rob was on his way.

So he got himself something hot and chocolaty to drink, with a lot of caffeine. And a blueberry-filled pastry that he was likely to end up wearing if he wasn't careful. Nothing for the ladies, because he was just a guy, out running errands or something, and had stopped for a snack.

Never break character, even when the scene falls apart or your partner forgets their lines. If nothing else, the director and producer will remember you for holding everything together, even as they put a little black mark in the book next to that other fool's name.

He was good at being Roberto Segura. That was a comfortable legend that even fit with the overall scale of things. Personal pilot for a woman with a lot of money and the desire to stay in Bennan for an extended vacation that only rarely bothered the resorts. Or her employees.

People tended to forget that the city was here, the tree they missed for the forest.

Rob settled in such a way that he was more or less facing Yankov, but clear across the room from the other agent.

From here, the man was in his early sixties. Well-preserved, though not as well as Jorge's timelessness. Also hadn't spent as much time and effort on plastic surgery as Jorge, but there were hints around the eyes and ears.

Trying to look younger, to stay in the game longer. Wasn't that Carlota's sin? Aging out of a role where she'd only been seen as a sexpot used to entrap enemy agents?

Always younger punks like Handsome Rob coming along to displace you as the money man folks went to when they needed results. The *Can't Shoot Straight Gang* had quietly filled that role for Miguel and the Service for more than a decade now, though they were all long in the tooth.

Mrs. Jones had moved on to dramatic roles, and no longer needed a martial arts gunslinger who could ride a motorcycle one-handed while engaging in a running firefight. Like Carlota, Mrs. Jones had reached an age where foolish audiences no longer believed that an older woman could be hot, smart, competent, and deadly.

All you had to do was compete with Roxy on a Hogan's Alley combat simulator some time to understand what a dumb idea that was.

However, there were younger women filling those roles. Younger agents replacing Roxy, Carlota, and even Emil Yankov.

Rob noshed on his pastry, getting it all over his hands but not his shirt as he considered the passage of time. He was already an assassin for the Service. That was the topmost layer as far as operatives went. He could look forward to maybe twenty more years of that if he survived.

Then what? On that day, he wouldn't even be as old as Roxy, or Carlota, or Mac were today. Would he be washed up? Forced to invent a new role? Carve out a new spot for himself?

Jorge had the *Can't Shoot Straight Gang*. Miguel had suggested more than once that he saw Handsome Rob building his own equivalent one of these days.

How long would Mac be able to continue turning every head in the room? Alicia handled the tech side of things better than just about anybody Rob had ever known.

If he was really serious, he'd need another shooter like Roxy. But much, much younger. That new chick coming up who was hungry and fresh. Mac could hold center stage like Jorge did for a while, but at most probably only for a decade, likely.

Longbow was the medic and his own kind of cover, as they'd found out on *6940 Draconis*, when the Governor had turned out to be a music fan.

Nigel on technical support. Which was a fancy way of saying armorer and explosives.

Rob wasn't sure what kind of team he might need to

build if they were going to have a dedicated ship like *Valencia Del Oro* and Raef as captain. Instead, he watched a complete stranger read a report out of an official-looking binder, one eye always popping up regularly.

Rob even let them make eye contact at one point, two harmless strangers in a coffee shop, both passing the time. He smiled at Emil Yankov as he took the man's measure, then nodded and went back to whatever daydreams Roberto Segura had when he wasn't being anybody else.

Probably something he should start cultivating now. Never want to get to that day when they pull you out of the field and retire you to a desk, like they'd done to Carlota, without being able to turn yourself into the sort of person who didn't crack under the stress.

Like she had.

Jorge had obviously seen it coming, and gone his own way. Loudly and with a martini glass that never seemed to be empty. Rob had still seen the man shoot.

And heard stories among the older combat instructors back at Puerto Peñasco.

Yeah, when this operation was done, he needed to get serious about building up a team, including Mac and Alicia for as long as they could handle it and wanted to play. And then figuring out what a fifty-year-old Handsome Rob did for a second act.

Who did he want to be when he grew up?

Rob didn't have a good answer, but his donut was done, so he wiped his hands, stood up, and smiled at the entire universe.

At least he knew what questions to ask, so that he didn't turn out like Emil Yankov or Carlota Rojas.

He tossed his napkin and empty cup into the bin, ignoring Yankov entirely, and moved to the front door, never once looking back. Just a guy whose break was over and who needed to get back to work.

He'd come to understand Emil Yankov's place in this game.

Carlota was next on his list.

24

MAC HAD SPENT HOURS WITH THE WOMAN, SO SHE HAD an even better understanding of who Carlota Rojas was now. Being in fingertip contact would do that.

Aged out. That was what they called models who reached that terrible, magical age where the photographers she had previously worked with no longer called. Whether it was twenty-two, thirty, or some other magical number, suddenly nobody wanted you.

Mac had seen it coming and gone several other directions instead, before ending up somehow back at something of a starting point, being the most beautiful woman in the room, any room, only this time as a cover for all the things she and Rob did.

Carlota had aged out and been thrown to the wolves.

Did the woman want to survive? That was the question Mac kept circling back to. This was a performance piece guaranteed to have an audience, but they were all sharks, waiting for you to fall into the water so they could eat you. Hungry gators, smiling just below the surface.

Was it all a terrible death wish? *Le Beau Geste?* The immortal gesture?

Nobody could know that but Carlota, and Mac was reasonably certain that even that woman hadn't come to a conclusion. Too much uncertainty in her, as Mac had been able to sense with her fingertips.

Carlota was alive, but it almost seemed to surprise the woman.

Did her endgame have a good ending?

Today, Mac was up in her room, relaxing. She'd spent time this morning down in the pool, swimming laps and working on her tan, just to stay in shape and in character. Many men and women watched her with covetous eyes, but none of them impressed her like Carlota had.

Or Rob did every time he looked at her. His eyes saw who she was, and lusted after her mind and soul as much as her body. It was a pity they were so far apart in age.

A knock at the door as she sat musing drew her back to the present. Mac rose and made sure everything was right as she moved to the door. Dressed for an afternoon of shopping or whatever, because Rob had been out spotting Yankov this morning and nobody knew what the play would be.

She checked the screen showing the hallway and it was Rob, so she unlocked the door and opened it.

He stepped in and closed it, then leaned over and kissed her. More than a simple hello kiss, at that. Much more. She wondered if they might end up back in the sleeping chamber, but he broke it off and smiled at her, moving past to the kitchen area and opening the refrigerator.

She watched him pull out a pitcher of orange juice and pour himself some, gesturing to see if she wanted any.

Mac shook her head and moved to the other side of the little peninsula counter to watch him.

"News?" she asked after a moment.

"I think so," he said.

"Do we need Alicia?" Mac pressed.

"Not yet."

Handsome Rob grinned at her, again like he was having ulterior motives and wanting to seduce her. Not that she'd mind. His seductions sometimes took hours.

"I went out and sat with Yankov in a donut shop after he left the publisher with the latest issue," Rob began finally. "Tried to take the man's measure in ways that Jorge taught me, rather than the agency."

"What did you find?" Mac asked, intrigued.

Jorge Royo was even better at understanding people than Rob. That man seemed to able to read their soul with a single glance, better than any psychologist's report.

"Carlota was put out to pasture because they thought she was too old," Rob nodded as he worked out details.

"I can understand that concept," Mac replied dryly.

Similar fears had kept her up at night, even before this mission had been sprung on her.

"Yankov has had work done." Rob turned serious. "Enough to look younger than he is, white hair and beard notwithstanding. And then I go back to people like Stansfield Brightmeadow-Gates, who almost got me killed."

"Stansfield?" Mac asked, blinking a little in surprise. "Why him?"

"He was offended at the passage of time," Rob said, surprising her even more. "That the Service had evolved, and no longer did things the old way. That Jorge and the Gang were needed because old methods weren't as useful."

"Okay?" Mac asked as a placeholder.

"We all grow up," Rob said in a serious voice. "The missions change because the personnel changes, but eventually we all get too old to do that thing we trained for and wanted to do more than anything."

Mac grunted rather than speak the obscenity on the tip of her tongue aloud.

"Exactly," Rob nodded, as if reading her mind. "At the end of the day, Carlota doesn't think she's too old to do this job. So far, I tend to agree with her, because she's been good enough to keep everyone running. If this is her, then we've just been utterly lucky. None of it was skill to find her, only to recognize that you might have stumbled over her and to not panic."

"So now what?" Mac asked.

They'd chewed this bone round and round.

"Option one, we let them kill her," Rob said, tapping a finger on the counter between them. When she started to object, he smiled. "Option two, we help her get away by blowing covers on folks like Yankov. Wouldn't be that hard to frame him for something and get the man arrested. Same with a half-dozen other folks we've encountered, like that one *Aquitaine* agent you recognized from the pictures Alicia captured."

"Madison Volante," Mac groused, remembering him from a reception where he'd nearly gotten punched in the jaw before he'd take no as an answer.

"Yes," Rob agreed. "*Wraith*. We could burn them all, quite easily. Ruin a whole swath of careers in espionage. Do to them what they did to Carlota."

Mac liked that option, but she was also willing to admit that she was cheering for Carlota Rojas to pull off her grand audacity, if only to make those men understand that women were more than the sum of their tits and asses. Miguel had never fallen into that trap, but he was an exception and Mac knew it.

"I get the impression that you have an Option Three," Mac said as Rob stood there grinning.

"What if she defects?" he asked. "You are her. What

would you do if I walked up and offered to smuggle you off planet, after mailing everything?"

"Won't work," Mac said instantly.

"No?"

"No. I need to die. And do it in such a way that they stop hunting for me," Mac said. "I need a corpse nobody will miss. Right shape and age. Unidentifiable because nobody has her true records. They need to kill me so they know that I've failed."

"Do they get to keep the rest of the manuscript?" Rob asked, eyes glittering.

"Yes," Mac decided. "That's how they know I'm dead. They managed to win the game. The parts already out there are gossip and speculation without those pages she held back that list dates and names. Rude, but not enough to send people to jail or bring down governments."

"And if I do rescue you and offer you a chance to go back to *Ramsey* and keep working?" Rob asked.

Mac felt a spike of adrenaline in the center of her stomach that hit almost as hard as a good orgasm.

"Staying in the game was all I ever wanted," Mac/Carlota whispered aloud. "If I'm dead, they stop looking for me, and I can really get my vengeance on them."

"Even working for *Lincolnshire*?" Rob asked.

"I want heads on stakes as a warning to future generations not to assume a woman field agent is worthless after she hits thirty," Mac/Carlota hissed terribly.

Rob nodded. He set his glass down and reached across the counter, touching her chin and turning it up as he leaned over to kiss her lightly on the lips. Again, the promise of hours of seduction. Later

Mac took a deep breath and broke cover. Or whatever you wanted to call it. Turned back into Esmeralda MacTavish aka Mac and not Carlota Rojas. It was like stepping out of a sauna into cool air as she let the mad heat of that woman's rage slip away.

"What do we need to do?" Mac asked, more herself again.

"Find her," Rob said.

"Then?"

"Convince her we mean business," Rob said.

Mac felt the smile erupt from the very bottom of her soul. Carlota was going to get to win.

Mac would see to it.

25

CARLOTA HAD CHOSEN TO TAKE IT EASY TONIGHT. SHE would stay at the hotel for a nice dinner and then return to her room with music and maybe a good vid.

Twice, she'd gotten lucky on her infrequent jaunts out, first winning all that money with Armand's help before allowing the man to consummate his seduction. Then stumbling across Erika at a black box theater.

If she had believed that she was going to survive all this, Carlota might even seek out the woman again. However, Carlota knew now that her days were numbered and decreasing rapidly.

They would find her eventually. Statistics favored them, not her. All she could do was stretch the game out long enough that her victory would eventually become a case study for the various intelligence agencies out there and how to deal with older agents.

Hopefully, not by kidnapping them and exiling them to some island where they could never escape, given the things they knew. She'd read fantastical stories with such a setting, prisoners who spent the entire series trying to get off the island and reclaim their real identity, rather than just being a number for the rest of their lives.

All she had to do was survive long enough that she won.

It was an intoxicating thought, as she checked herself in the mirror. Brown hair, brown eyes, brown skin. Normal enough to pass in the general population of *Borlait* without standing out. Tonight, she'd put on a long dress in a burnished gold that seemed to dance like flames around her.

Sometimes, the image in the mirror looked like she was being burned at the stake, but tonight, she felt like a phoenix, descending into ashes in order to be reborn. It was a hopeless wish, but she would achieve some measure of immortality from it all.

And her revenge on Grendel Montague. Never lose sight of that worthy goal.

He might think he'd won when she was dead, but if she could just stretch that out far enough, the truth would come out. Chapter Twelve would burn him personally.

Carlota touched up her makeup and checked her roots. Probably need to do them up again in a few days, but not yet. She had pills that mostly kept them dark enough that it didn't come in underneath like a white helmet.

She slipped a stun pistol into her clutch like usual and made her way to the door, pausing to look around once.

After all, every time she walked out that door, there was a growing chance that she would never come back.

Tonight, she was feeling especially morbid. Vulnerable, perhaps. Almost enough to try her luck and see if there was another Armand or Erika out there. Maybe even Erika herself, though Carlota had no idea how she might track the woman down short of walking up to her door and knocking.

And stepping out into the lights of the city to go hunting opened her up to all the hunters out there.

Not worth it. Tonight.

As she closed the door behind her, Carlota knew that tomorrow might make her desperate enough to change her mind.

26

Rob had brought Alicia with him, leaving Mac as their backup on this one.

It was weird, traveling with the younger woman. Alicia was brilliant, but not trained as a field agent. Her nervousness left him a little on edge, but she was handling herself well.

Just not up to what he was used to with Mac.

They entered the hotel lobby hand in hand, each carrying an overnight bag like a young couple sneaking away for a weekend. She was only a few years older than him at thirty-one, but he felt ancient standing next to her. Part of that was being used to holding Mac's hand, where Alicia made him feel like something of a dirty old man.

Weird. And something he needed to work on. Especially if he was going to build his own gang like Jorge had. No woman got anything but Jorge's complete attention.

They made their way to the front desk.

"May I help you?" the young woman asked.

"Reservations for Carlyle," he said, pulling out the

documents Alicia had printed when he'd laid out this mission.

"Yes, sir, Sri Carlyle," the woman nodded. "I see that you're already fully checked in and just need your keys."

He watched her pull out a pair of white cards and program them for the door. Alicia had been able to handle it all remotely, but he didn't want to have her try their security remotely. Too easy to blow his own cover at that point, since he had been traveling a bit openly at their other hotel.

"There you go," the woman continued, handing him an envelope. "Room six-twenty-seven. Did you have any questions?"

"No, we're good," Rob said.

He turned to Alicia and noted the nervousness in her eyes, so he leaned down and kissed her. Different kind of shock now, but it distracted her until they got into the elevator.

She was still holding his hand like a life preserver, and leaned into him some. Rob wondered if she'd take him up on the offer from the other night. It had been there in her eyes then, and never far since.

At the same time, she was a stone professional and he appreciated that. As far as he knew, she liked boys, but that wasn't his concern. She would say something, or she wouldn't.

For now, they were running an operation, with Mac nearby in a delivery truck Alicia had rented for them for a few days.

The elevator delivered them to the seventh floor, the entire ground level being facilities rather than rooms. Rob found his way to the left, Alicia still holding his hand like she was drawing strength from it.

The doors had a little card pad next to them. Flash the

badge at it from close by and a resonant magnetic field matched, causing the locks to retract.

Easy enough to spoof, but they were all wired into a central system, so that anomalies would trigger alarms.

Which was why he needed somebody like Alicia handy. Rob could pick locks. He could locate a maintenance uniform that would let him pop the cover off a panel to get inside and disable it, but that introduced a whole series of escalating risks.

Better to introduce a deadly genius cryptographer and ask her to commit warfare on the hotel's security system. Rob knew who he'd bet on in that scenario. That was why he'd asked for the woman in the first place.

They got inside. Rob moved to the only bed and put his bag down, then shifted to the farthest end of the room to get out of Alicia's way.

Both bags contained all her gear. Even then, she'd had to pair it down to just a few things, rather than some of the toys she'd left downtown.

Rob pulled up a chair and settled, watching Alicia do her magic.

It was all explainable magic. Technical terms she and Mac could bandy about, but he wasn't fooled. Both of those women were operating at a level where few other humans could even understand, let alone challenge. That was why the Service employed them.

Like downtown, she pulled out a wire and hunted down the plug in the wall before opening her clamshell. Wired signals were harder to detect, harder to jam, and impossible for someone else to listen to except from inside the system.

Alicia sat cross-legged on the bed with her clamshell computer on her lap, tapping keys slowly. Almost individually. It was out of his hands at this point.

Rob fell into a meditative state. She'd warned him that it might take hours before she could crack into their systems, since nobody knew how good they might be.

The profanity that escaped her lips opened his eyes.

Alicia blushed so dark she looked like she was about to faint.

"You might have been able to do this one on your own," she muttered.

"I hardly know what I'm doing with stuff like that," Rob retorted.

"Yeah, I know," she grimaced. "Amateur hour here. It's like they built this place forty years ago and haven't upgraded their security protocols since."

"They might not have," Rob pointed out. "How many people would be here instead of one of the resorts?"

Her eyes blinked wide open in surprise.

"Oh," she replied.

"So, you own them, like you do everywhere else we go?" he grinned.

She matched his grin now.

"What would you like to know?" she asked.

"Reservations data," he said. "Find me all candidates that might be Carlota or Helen. Assume she's been here at least a month, is staying alone, and go from there."

"On it," Alicia said.

As her attention dropped back to her screen, he sent Mac a note.

In and in. Room 718. – R

The code was simple enough. Subtract one from the first and last numbers. Add one to the middle. It was a public message. No reason to tell anybody anything, if they happened to intercept it.

That would be Mac's cue to park her van in the

underground garage and ride up to join them with another bag, this one filled with his gear.

You never knew when you'd have to unleash some mayhem. He'd prefer being armed sufficient unto the task, just in case.

27

Mac heard the chirp of her comm and checked the note from Rob. She'd been more concerned about Alicia's performance than he had, but they'd also talked briefly about the future.

Their future, in the context of another *Can't Shoot Straight Gang*, where she filled the role of a beautiful woman chameleon who could be thirty as easily as sixty. While she was nowhere near as deadly as Roxy, Mac didn't think that Rob needed that from her. She could still shoot as good as any of the Service's regular field agents.

And those standards weren't low.

Alicia had made a concerted effort over the last year at eating healthier, exercising more, and stomping past those old physical fitness requirements that she'd just edged across previously. The woman would never be slinky and beautiful, but she was getting more conventionally attractive every day.

They could be a dedicated team. If that was what Mac wanted.

She slipped the van into gear and considered how much Rob had gotten inside her own mind. He had to know that

Miguel would continue to let her do this, but that his replacement would most likely forbid it.

Maybe that was why Handsome had gotten serious about making them into a team? They couldn't just replace her at that point. Not easily, anyway.

Mac shook her head. Too much time in Carlota's mindspace. She knew that. Had dreamed where the two of them had to face down an entire mob of other agents, all young and beautiful, male and female.

Fear of being left behind.

She drove the van inward and concentrated on the fact that they would not be allowed to win.

Whoever that metaphorical *they* happened to be.

Could they rescue Carlota? She didn't know. At some point, the siren call of using high explosives and flammables to destroy it all would get into any woman's head. Hopefully, Carlota could be redeemed.

At this point, Mac was certain that Helen was Carlota. If not, then they were about to blow their own covers.

Rob had contingency plans. None of them were pleasant, but this was an industry that went where normal people hesitated. Rob would take someone down, if Helen turned out to be more like Mac as another chimeric hunter looking for the elusive Carlota.

And, God have mercy on her soul, Mac would help. In cold blood, even.

The van hit the ramp down and she paid close attention to how they would get out later. A car chase was the worst possible outcome here, probably. The van wasn't the sort of vehicle she or Rob would have chosen for such a thing.

Mac got lucky and found a spot on the first level below ground. It went down another three, if you needed it. She even had a spot wide enough that she could press a bit close on the driver's side and have extra space in back for the side door to slide open for access.

She parked, secured everything, and grabbed the suitcase that Handsome Rob had retrieved from the ship. It was heavy, which was why it had rollers on one side. Rob wanted access to the same sorts of firepower that Alicia had brought. Metaphorical in her case. Literal in his.

It was late in the afternoon. Folks would mostly be checked in unless they were traveling some great distance. At the same time, a little too early for dinner, so the parking garage was practically empty. She rode up the elevator by herself to six, then remembered that the numbers were weird here.

Up one more, she found the door and knocked.

Rob opened a crack, then pulled it the rest of the way and gestured her in.

Inside, Alicia had taken over the bed to open a couple of notebooks and two clamshell computers. Rob moved her case to the desk by the window and Mac found herself trailing him.

She watched him pull out a class four pulse pistol and check the charge pack. A holster joined it, then he drew out the class three he carried for her.

Like Rob, she could shoot most weapons. This one just fit her hand better.

Mac silently stripped off her jacket and put the holster under her arm even as Rob was doing the same thing.

She knew shit was serious when he pulled out a pair of stun grenades and slipped them into his pocket when he put his jacket back on. He'd saved her ass before by bringing those sorts of things into a bar once. And using them.

Hopefully, it wouldn't be necessary. They could have a simple conversation and determine who Helen really was.

"I've got her," Alicia announced breathlessly.

Mac and Rob both turned back to stare at the woman.

"She's on ten," Alicia said. "Ten-oh-two. Different name. Only person that suits the search pattern."

"Does security have a picture of her on file, if she's been here that long?" Mac asked.

Alicia started in surprise, then began typing.

Anyone who was going to be someplace long enough would get filed, just so security didn't end up with false positives if they kept seeing the same person hanging around. That caused their paranoia to beep.

"Oh, wow," Alicia said.

Mac moved around Rob so she could look at the screen. She felt Rob's breath on her ear.

Helen. Who might also be Carlota Rojas. A woman in over her head and uncertain how she might get out.

Mac didn't think the woman she'd taken to bed had given up at life. And she'd spent hours being intimate.

But that wasn't the same thing as knowing how to survive.

Mac wasn't sure how she could have gotten herself out of such a mess.

Would she have even gotten into it? Was that Miguel's worst nightmare, that she might go rogue?

At least Mac understood now just what a hunt of that magnitude would look like.

And how little chance she stood of surviving it.

"That's her," Mac confirmed, even as Alicia and Rob nodded. "Now what?"

"Now, we go pay her a visit," Rob said grimly. "And find out who she's working for."

Mac nodded.

Helen was another agent like them.

Now, the truth would come out.

28

CARLOTA FINISHED AN EXCELLENT STEAK AND TRIED TO decide if she wanted dessert, or if she should forgo it tonight. If they were going to kill her eventually, it made sense to just give in to decadence.

On the other hand, she wasn't ready to be dead, regardless of what Montague and all his worthless ilk thought on the matter.

She sighed with regret and passed it up, just having some decaf coffee, heavy with cream, to settle everything. More than once as she ate, Carlota had reconsidered going hunting. Slipping into town and seeing if she could get as lucky as Armand and Erika.

Something. Anything to fill that vacant hole of loneliness in her chest that seemed to be growing.

A pit that would eventually swallow her whole, leaving nothing but what memories remained in the minds of the ones that killed her.

Would it be enough? Would her sacrifice mean that some future agent wasn't patted on the head and put out to pasture, just because she was a woman? After all, many men stayed in the game right up to the point that they had to retire due to age.

Why not her? Why not any of them?

She was almost ready to just mail the rest of the manuscript off. Burn everything down immediately and be done with it.

Know that she had destroyed the man, before he had gotten to her.

But she couldn't. It would be an admission that they'd won. That she'd had to break the very rules she had established at the beginning.

That would be chocked up in her mind as a loss.

Not the way she wanted to die.

Carlota suppressed a growl and rose, maintaining her elegance as she did. The night was early, but she'd simply been too restless to stay up in her room for any longer. There was a bottle of wine up there. Most likely, she'd have a heavy glass, then watch some mindless comedy for a while, hoping to unwind enough to sleep.

That might be a losing battle as well. She would fight that war when it came.

The staff were pleasant as always, which helped. She made her way back to the lobby and the elevators, still fuming some, but uncertain as to how she might resolve everything.

Carlota was finally willing to admit, as she entered the elevator, that she didn't really want to die. She'd been so wound up in her revenge that she'd forgotten the first maxim of revenge.

Dig two graves when you set out.

One for Montague. One for her. *Borlait* would be her grave. Bennan itself. All that would remain behind were the legends that would accumulate around however many chapters of the manuscript made it out before they caught her.

It was what it was. She had dug this grave, she just hadn't realized it at the time.

Carlota sighed.

The elevator stopped midway and the doors opened. A man and a woman were entering.

The woman gasped.

Carlota shifted into full wakefulness and realized that it was Erika herself standing there.

Then the man shoved her backwards against the wall and pressed the barrel of a pistol into the bone between her breasts.

"Do not move," he growled quietly as the door closed.

29

Rob was back on any of those damned combat ranges that the engineering staff set up at headquarters. Every Friday they went to work, tearing down the old Hogan's Alley and building a new one from scratch, just so that agents training had something different every Monday.

The woman in charge of them was also something of a friendly sadist in her designs, but it kept Rob and the field agents hopping.

Like now.

The elevator doors opened and he stepped in, processing as he moved that Carlota/Helen just happened to be aboard, by herself, and not paying attention.

The class four practically teleported itself into his hand and Rob moved directly into the woman, pinning her back with one hand on a shoulder and the gun socketed into her cleavage. There was nowhere she could go to evade him that didn't involve getting shot dead, because breasts or chin would hang up on the weapon itself long enough for him to pull the trigger.

Roxy had taught him that one. Didn't work as well on

most men, for obvious reasons, but that was why the hand went to the shoulder, gripping.

"Do not move," Rob instructed the woman, not taking his eyes off the panic that was just starting to settle into her eyes.

He felt Mac enter and slide to one side. The doors closed.

"Hit the stop button," Rob said aloud.

Mac did and the elevator ceased moving as soon as it had started.

Carlota/Helen was a professional. She didn't scream. Didn't struggle. Didn't seem to even be breathing.

"Believe it or not, we're here to help," Rob said, allowing a smile on his face, even as he had her pinned. "Assuming you are who I think you are. What cover name would you like to use, Helen?"

The woman flinched. Mac reached in and pulled the little purse out of her unresisting hands.

Helen just stared at him, her eyes blinking too rapidly as she tried to process what had just happened.

A lightning bolt. That was what it was. He'd been all set to go upstairs and have Alicia remotely override the door lock so they could rush in and surprise the woman if she was in the room.

Five minutes earlier, and they might have been storming an empty space. That would have been fine. He'd have waited up for her.

Hopefully, she wouldn't have been out all night again.

He'd have waited up for her then, too.

"Helen is fine," she whispered, slowly drawing strength into herself. "What happens next?"

"Next, we verify your bonafides," Rob said grimly. "I have one sure-fire way to do that. Then I have a whole raft of questions for you, Helen."

"Okay," the woman said, still not entirely present but coming back to herself.

Rob kept the rudeness of his pistol in place.

"I would like to think that you have a plan for surviving all this, and that we're just along for the ride," Rob continued. "Am I right, Helen?"

She slumped. A little. Not much. Enough.

The woman was expecting to die when it was all done.

"Who are you really, Helen?" he asked.

"You know," she murmured. "That's why you're here."

"I need you to say it," he pressed.

"*Hummingbird*," she breathed with another slump.

"Thank you," Rob said to her. "I'm going to put my pistol away now. We're going up to your room and talk. I think I can save you."

There was no greater feeling in the entire universe than watching hope dawn in somebody's eyes. He got to see it happen with Helen who might be Carlota Rojas.

Rob took a full step back and put away the class four. He nodded to Mac, but she'd never drawn hers. Instead, she pressed the button and the elevator began to rise again.

It opened on eleven and Rob took Helen by the elbow, like a date, and had Mac trail them with the stunner she'd found in Helen's purse. He took the key for himself.

Helen wasn't resisting, but he figured it was only a matter of time before she caught up with the present tense and did something. He'd surprised her at some sort of mental and emotional low moment, and taken advantage of the woman.

He would apologize later.

They got to her door and Rob keyed it open, practically dragging Helen inside, but she really didn't have much choice. In her mind, he could see where she had correctly identified him as a foreign agent, hunting her like all the others.

She just hadn't placed him yet geographically.

Rob looked around the room and put her on the bed. Mac was covering the door. Rob pulled a chair away from the desk and watched the woman flinch as he did.

Not at him. At where he was standing.

Rob paused to look around. Desk with a stack of empty mailing envelopes and nothing else. Chest of drawers off to one side. Suitcase tucked into the corner out of the way.

He pulled out his comm and dialed Alicia.

"Here," she replied instantly.

"We accidentally stumbled into the woman in the elevator," he said simply. "We're inside her room right now, having a chat. Please keep watch on everything."

"Right." And she cut the line.

Alicia already owned the hotel's systems. That included security lines. If anyone called them, she would know as soon as it happened and notify him.

What he would do still remained to be seen. He did have the grenades in his pocket like terrible eggs, ready to hatch out into mayhem.

"Helen," Rob said. "*Hummingbird.* I think you are somebody important. A particular woman who is causing a bunch of other people a lot of stress."

"Other people?" she asked, her voice finally finding strength.

"I'm not here to stop you," Rob grinned. "If anything, my bosses would like your book to come out. They sent me because they understood that all these folks running around chasing you would make it much easier for me to mark them and start circulating their pictures later so we could burn them when we needed to. Or maybe consider doubling them."

Her eyes were cagey now. Canny. Sharp.

This was not a woman to be trifled with. Certainly not overlooked, unless you were a complete dumbass.

Rob supposed that Roxy had made sure he got over any of those stupid ideas he might have had. As had Mac.

At the same time, he couldn't see *Salonnia* or *Fribourg* getting that. *Aquitaine* wasn't nearly as sexist, except that they'd apparently sent *Wraith*, and Mac had a low opinion of the man.

All of them chauvinist pigs, it seemed.

That left him.

"What do you want?" Helen demanded in a firm, hard voice.

She didn't move. Mac would stun her as soon as she did. Helen seemed to respect that. Hopefully, she saw herself standing by the door, were the situation reversed.

"I would like to confirm that you are in fact Carlota Rojas," Rob said, finally speaking that magical name out loud for the first time in front of her. "Then I would like to hear your plan for how you intended to survive this amazing shitshow you've unleashed on the various intelligence underworlds of the galactic arm."

He was smiling as he spoke. After all, Rob could simply walk away this minute and go home with all the information he'd accumulated on the many folks running around chasing after Helen. He even knew who Emil Yankov was now, and could write an entire psychological dossier on the man to fill in any gaps that existed in the one back home.

Proper intelligence work wasn't what Rob did. Those folks spent months and years slowly digging up clues in reports, leaks, and rumors. They watched folks do things that opened them up to blackmail, and then nailed them with it. They doubled agents who would pass along documents for ideological or financial reasons.

Kinetic solutions were only necessary in situations where

everything had gone wrong. Or when you needed to remove someone who was a threat that could not be removed any other way.

He could go home tomorrow and the intelligence operatives would buy him a beer and spend months milking him for tidbits that would let them go after all these other spies.

It was good.

Helen watched him like a cobra facing down a mongoose. Not an inapt comparison. She was deadly. He was fast.

And could always walk away with clean hands and a clean conscience.

"What are you going to do?" Helen asked. "If I was?"

"I'm going to call you Carlota," Rob decided. "I'm going to treat you like you are. If you aren't, then we have a problem and I'll deal with that as needed. In the meantime, I want answers. You can provide them, or I'll burn you to everyone on the planet and let them decide what to do with you. Is that clear enough?"

Both women gasped in shock. Not surprising. Both were field agents. Assassin required a different mindset. A willingness to execute somebody for no better reason than their name was next on some list.

Handsome Rob knew he was a borderline sociopath. You had to be. They reinforced that, having him dance along that edge.

Normal people wouldn't kill someone in cold blood.

He let Helen/Carlota see the cold death lingering in his eyes. Mac was behind him, but she'd already seen it. Touched it. Known it intimately, as it were.

He was a killer. Carlota could be a victim. Or someone he rescued.

Her choice.

He waited. She watched him. Then Mac. Then him again.

Rob waited. In the back of his head, he might have heard the music that the fakir plays to draw the cobra up out of the basket.

"You aren't here to kill me?" Helen finally asked.

"Nope," Rob said. "Worst, you piss me off enough that I tell everyone else where to find you, but you'd have to be working at it for that outcome to arrive."

She flinched under his words, but he was trying to grind her down. Anyone who set out on the path Carlota Rojas had was already a hard, dangerous person. A woman with no more fucks left to give.

He could honor that, but it wasn't going to turn his head.

"In the suitcase," Helen said, nodding to the corner.

Rob nodded and rose, moving around the chair so he was never in Mac's line of fire if she needed to take Helen down.

"Anything I need to know before I open it?" he said without touching.

"No," Helen said. "There is a false bottom sewn in. The seam is along the top when upright."

She seemed exhausted. Deflated.

It might still be an act. Rob pulled gloves from his pocket and moved the suitcase to the desk, standing and facing her across it.

He gave her one last moment to warn him, then turned to Mac.

"If something happens to me, I want her dead," he announced calmly.

Mac flinched, but she nodded. He was in charge here. She worked for him, in spite of the age difference.

Assassin. Field Agent. Alicia was just an Analyst.

His game. His call.

Rob locked eyes with Helen and undid the flap holding

the thing closed. It came away without any issues, revealing a hollow interior. The weight was wrong if it was.

He found the seam. A loose thread that seemed extremely heavy.

"Do I pull the thread?" he asked.

"Pull the flap," she replied. "It will come away with a little effort."

Rob grunted and nodded. He found a handhold and tugged. The thread slipped back through holes and he found the pocket she'd mentioned.

Inside, he found paper. Rob pulled it out.

Looked like the manuscript, halfway buried under a crap-ton of cash in bundles. Big bills bundled. A lot of them.

Methodically, he set the money off to one side, noting that it was all Cedi bills. *Salonnian* cash. Stupid amounts of it, which was always a useful thing in this business.

The stack of papers was what he wanted though, contained in another mailing envelope that was open at one end.

He slid the stack out, half a mind concentrated on Helen in case she moved, flinched, or spoke.

The contents came free and he put them on the desk. Randomly flipping, Rob confirmed everything.

And won a bet with himself over a pair of names she'd left out of Chapter Three by withholding that one page until the end.

With great care, he put it all back together, sliding it into the envelope and then walking over where he could toss it onto the bed close to Carlota.

She really was Carlota Rojas. That was the manuscript that had stirred up so many hornet nests around here.

"So, Carlota," Rob said as he sat again. "Now what?"

30

CARLOTA WATCHED THE MAN, STUNNED UTTERLY MUTE.

"Who are you?" she finally whispered.

His smile was warm. Charming. The sort of thing she'd seen on Armand. Or Erika, currently guarding the door. Who wasn't going to be an Erika, obviously.

"*The Lincolnshire Guardia Civil Interior,*" the man replied.

Lincolnshire Intelligence, she automatically translated in her head. The bad guys, more often than not.

Carlota could see them enjoying the spectacle.

"I'm Rob," he said casually.

Rob. He didn't look like a Rob. And yet he did.

"Rob," she nodded. "I've met Erika."

"She'll be Erika for now," Rob said. "We're back to you. What are your plans from here?"

"Do I have any?" Carlota asked, trying not to let her rage take control of her.

To come so close, then have it all fall apart at the end. And to *Lincolnshire*, at that. Not even the Bureau or Imperial Intelligence.

"You have many," this Rob was saying. "I like the fits you've given everybody, and have no reason to stop you."

"How did you find me?" Carlota finally demanded, staring at Erika.

"Luck," Rob said, Erika remaining mute. "But I manufacture my luck."

The words drew her eyes back to this Rob person. Carlota found her mouth saying the word *manufacture* without any noise.

"That's right," he nodded, still serenely in control. "When your introduction and first chapter arrived on *Ramsey*, the boss called me to read it and then asked if I thought we could do anything about it."

She watched him, intrigued. His smile was engaging, and not the false smile of a torturer playing a long game of good cop.

"I manufacture my luck," he repeated, nodding over his shoulder to Erika.

Rob looked thirty. Erika was Carlota's age, give or take, so old enough to be this pup's mother. And yet, they had a casualness—a respect—about them that suggested more-than-occasional lovers. Most men that age had no clue how to treat a mature woman.

Did this Rob fellow know what he was doing?

"I told my boss that I needed Erika," Rob continued. "That she would be able to think like you. Act like you. Get inside your head and see things that none of the others out there chasing you would see. And I also had luck handed to me."

"How so?" Carlota asked, even more intrigued.

This was absolutely nothing like an interrogation. More like three friends having tea. She could stretch that to include Erika. They'd been…*intimate*.

Never with Rob, though Carlota could see where he was

studying her like an attractive woman, and not as another asset. Or a prisoner to be wrung dry and discarded.

A woman. A dangerous woman, from the carefulness of how he moved around her.

Respect.

"*Fribourg* sent Emil Yankov to chase you," Rob said.

Carlota flinched at the thought of the Grand Old Man of Imperial Intelligence himself coming after her. How had he missed so far?

More of Rob's manufactured luck?

"*Aquitaine* sent *Wraith*, a gentleman known usually as Madison Volante," Rob continued.

Again, big guns hunting her.

Some of her confusion must have shown.

"If I suggested both men were hopeless male chauvinist pigs, I don't think I'd be doing them a proper justice," Rob laughed. "They go far beyond that level into truly petty. Probably on a par with your former boss Grendel Montague."

She couldn't help the growl that escaped. Rob was obviously a fairly senior spy for *Lincolnshire* to know those names and be able to use them casually in conversation.

What did he want from her?

"What about you?"

"I saw Erika on that page," Rob sobered. "In that first chapter. She could have written it. She could have been in your shoes, but for some of her own manufactured luck. And mine, when she saved my life the first time."

First time? That suggested more than once. Were they partners in addition to being lovers? Lovers in addition to being partners? Both seemed to describe the two of them.

Erika had a male partner who respected her. Trusted her. Relied on her publicly.

Carlota had a bunch of pigs she intended to burn.

Rob's smile got broader as her face grew confused. She couldn't help that. This woman had gotten all the things that Carlota wanted.

Including respect.

"I asked the boss to let me bring Erika, because I figured that she could track you better than any of the men they sent," Rob said calmly. "When the two of you stumbled into each other, she raised a red flag and we started digging into who you might be. Until just now, I figured that you were another Erika that somebody else had brought along to help understand their quarry, but I think that everybody else was just after any woman of close to the right age to hunt. So we're back to the first question, Carlota. How does it all end?"

He wasn't threatening to shoot her this minute. Or turn her in. It almost felt like an academic question, because he really didn't care all that much.

How could he not?

"The game has rules," she found herself saying, calmed by the man. "Each week, I'll send out another chapter, now that everyone is here and chasing me."

He nodded, pensive but not interrupting as she spoke. Yet another point in his favor.

"The ones off-planet are sent priority," Carlota continued. "Local are send fourth class, so that they all arrive around the same time. How did you find Yankov?"

"He walked right into the office of your local publisher and apparently threatened the man," Rob said. "Then, to play good cop, is paying him enough cash to hire a temp for the next couple of months, even though they only need her one day per week. He came in to pick up the most recent copy and I was able to make him."

"Just like that?"

"Nobody around here knows me," Rob shrugged in a

cute way. "And I wasn't trying to find you so that I could stop you. It was easier to track everyone else because they never considered that they might be prey here."

Smart move. More *manufactured luck*, she supposed.

"Back to you," he volleyed the conversation expertly. "What happens?"

"Eventually, I mail the last chapter," Carlota breathed heavily. "And I win."

"Then what?"

Then what? The question that had been plaguing her for days.

What was there to say? Then she tried to hide and eventually somebody recognized her and they killed her. If she was lucky.

There were worse fates at this point. Being held captive by a pair of *Lincolnshire* agents rated high.

"Can I share a thought?" Rob asked, not waiting for her to nod before continuing. "I am willing to bet that you never thought you'd make it that far. Am I right?"

She nodded, unable to speak now with the deadly accuracy she'd seen the man evince.

"The big players want you, dead or prisoner," he said. "*Salonnia* will kill you for this. *Fribourg* probably as well, though Yankov might want to crack open your skull to dredge out everything he can get. *Aquitaine* is in that latter category."

"What about *Lincolnshire*?" Carlota demanded quietly.

"The boss sent me to take pictures of enemy agents," he grinned. "To ruin their careers as spies. I didn't think anybody would find you except by the random luck of a stringer on some street corner happening to recognize you walking by and calling someone. I didn't bring those sorts of resources to *Borlait*. That you and Erika ran into each other is one of those legends that the old farts can't tell the kids because nobody would believe that it wasn't an old fish story."

"So you aren't here to take me in and torture me?" Carlota asked, at once insulted and also maybe relieved.

She could enjoy the memories with Erika and not sully them as being part of an operation. No more than they had been. A most pleasant one.

"Actually, I'm here to ask if you want help," Rob said. "If not, I'll head home eventually. Maybe after you're done. Maybe sooner, if Yankov or someone gets lucky."

What?

"What?"

"On the other hand, if you wanted help, we're here to offer it," he said, nodding back to Erika. "What can we offer?"

"They'll kill me when they find me, Rob," Carlota reminded the man.

"Not if you're already dead," he smiled.

Carlota blinked, shocked to silence at the concept. The man had the audacity to smile at her.

"Go on," she managed to whisper.

Was there a way that didn't involve needing that second grave?

So he explained it to her.

Carlota listened, rapt.

31

MAC FOLLOWED ROB BACK TO THE ROOM THAT HE AND Alicia were supposedly staying in. The woman had been listening to the entire conversation silently while recording it.

"Will it work?" Mac asked as the door closed.

She hadn't been willing to confront him in front of Carlota.

Rob shrugged.

"A lot of it hinges on her, but I think she wants to survive," he said. "She might pack up and run as soon as we're out of sight, in which case I will retract my offer and we go back to identifying everyone else on the gameboard for Miguel. Eventually, they kill her. She can't run far enough to escape the sorts of shit that they will unleash on her when those last two chapters come out in print."

"And you'll just let them?" Mac found herself demanding.

Alicia glanced up at the tone of Mac's voice. Rob turned to face her, stepping close enough that Mac could punch him if she wanted.

"She's here because nobody respected that woman's

brains, savvy, competence, or deadliness, Mac," he snarled quietly. "The only thing I can offer her is that respect. To let her go out as a professional. Anything else and I'm taking something critical away from her. That I'm telling her I don't think she's good enough to be an agent in the field anymore. At that point, I'm no better than Yankov or Montague."

She recoiled from the sudden vehemence in his voice. Then she placed it. He saw Carlota in the exact same way he looked at her. Or Roxy. Mature women who most men overlooked because they were dumb-asses. Would discount, because her boobs weren't as perky as they used to be. The skin wasn't as fine. The curves were more solid.

They only saw the shell.

Rob had assumed everything inside the woman was at least as good an agent as him.

Respect. That had been the word that Carlota had loaded with the most emotion as they spoke. The one Rob just repeated.

Mac blinked. She relaxed and smiled.

Then she stepped fully into the man and kissed him, which served as the best surprise, feeling him flinch as her arms came up around him to pull those muscles against her.

"Hey, if you two are going to need the bed, we're getting a second room," Alicia called out.

Mac felt herself blush hard as she stepped back. Rob was almost as flustered. They both turned, one arm around the other, to look at Alicia.

Mac felt like a teenager who'd just been caught making out by her parents. Alicia's smile didn't help. Mac felt the blush darken even more.

"So, I don't have any indications that she's about to bail on us," Alicia said. "What's next?"

"You need to sit in the middle of your web here tonight," Rob was saying to her. "I can sleep on the floor so you two can have the bed. Tomorrow, hopefully we'll hear from Helen what she wants to do about it all. Right now, I think I need a glass of wine to unwind from all that. Did you want to join me or have room service?"

Mac squeezed his side and waited for Alicia.

"I'll get something delivered," the woman said. "Can you two take it somewhere else for a while? I feel like your mom or something equally icky."

Mac laughed and turned back to the door.

If Carlota went for it—Helen as everyone had agreed to keep calling her—then tomorrow a whole new operation would start up. One at least as good as anything that Jorge Royo had come up with recently.

Something as memorable as the *Can't Shoot Straight Gang*.

32

Rob had broken into a lot of strange places in his time. Committed all manner of crimes getting into and out of government buildings. This one had to be in the top three for overall weirdness.

He turned to Mac as they studied the place over there. Right now, they were just sort of trespassing after dark in a public park. Two lovers maybe looking for a little privacy, although anyone looking at how they were dressed would call the cops immediately.

Dark gray and mottled in such a way that you turned invisible when you stopped moving in dim light. Knit caps, with her hair braided under double first. Armed not quite to the teeth, but more stunners than you really needed for something like this.

He had the class four under his arm because he'd rather have it and not need it than need it and not have it.

"You ready?" he asked her.

Mac grinned, leaned in and kissed him, then nodded. Rob grinned back and moved out of the last line of trees to the cyclone fence that marked the edge of the forest where it backed up against the city government complex.

He considered it fortunate that his target tonight was nowhere close to the regional motor pool. That place was lit up round the clock, bright enough that he could pick it out on the horizon from here. Instead, they were over with the medical offices.

He was pretty sure breaking into the morgue to steal a body would compete with any of the crazy shit he'd done before this.

"Standing by," he said into the open comm.

The unit was low-powered. Maybe a mile of effective range in the open. He and Mac had placed a base unit back in the trees where it would send a boosted signal, deeply encrypted, to another unit Alicia had had him install earlier on a comm line way on the other edge of the park.

"All signals nominal," Alicia said.

Even in the open, you spoke in an underhanded code that didn't immediately alert someone hearing them. She was monitoring a variety of emergency bands for traffic, in case they set off an alarm.

He nodded to Mac and approached the wire itself. Bolt cutters made short work of the wire and didn't generate any sort of power signature a scanner somewhere might react to. Quickly, he cut three feet vertically and then three across. Mac pulled it back and he slipped through before holding it for her.

A simple plastic strap had just enough strength to hold it closed in place, from any distance looking like it hadn't been cut.

"Through and in," Mac said over the comm.

No response was a good one, so they looked over the back yard of the morgue. Bushes in places, but planted to add color rather than to block anything. A concrete slab patio with picnic tables where folks could eat their lunch outside on a nice day. Just enough lights on the outside of the building to see things.

Rob pulled a scanner unit from his pocket and slowly panned it across the rear of the various buildings around here, looking for short-range signals that would notice trespassers. Most places that had them would use one of about three commercial styles, but Bennan was too cheap.

Or they were off right now.

He nodded to Mac and walked forward slowly but upright, like a guy out for a midnight stroll. She walked beside him. Maybe they'd been out back necking, in case somebody looked out a window. Not a threat.

Not an attack. Heaven forbid.

Just two people walking up to the back of the dark building. It helped that all the lights were off inside, save for hallway lights spilling into offices. He led them to the rear door that Alicia's research had found for him earlier. Not the one into the garage, but storage anyway. Like everything else, it had basic, commercial keypads with a screen where you could move a fob close to be read.

Designed to keep out random strangers and not much more. Who needed to break into the morgue anyway? Well, he supposed folks looking for narcotics they could sell might, but crime and vagrancy wasn't nearly the problem on *Borlait* that it was elsewhere.

There were always jobs going wanting, because there weren't enough people to fill them. If you wanted to work, someone would hire you off the street.

He pulled out a multitool with all sorts of options and got the chisel-tip screwdriver. Perfect to pop the faceplate off the unit so he could get inside. Commercial unit. Lowest bidder deal. Cheap stuff.

He handed it to Mac and pulled a pocket light to study

things inside. One quick touch with the metal head and the door buzzed and thumped.

Mac pulled it open then handed him back the plate.

"That's done," he said casually to the night.

"All systems nominal."

Excellent. Their one great fear had been that the security might be wired to an extra alarm. If it went off, Alicia should hear it.

Of course, if they had it directly routed somehow, the first indication of trouble might be a car dropping out of the sky to investigate a door opening.

Likely followed by a shootout of some sort. And a blown cover.

Or at least a ruined operation. Wouldn't be the end of the world, but they'd have to find a different way to save Helen's life.

Rob was pretty sure she wanted to live at this point.

As opposed to dragging him down with her. That was always a possibility as well.

They slipped in the building. Just enough lights to see clearly. He let the door close quietly behind him, not seeing any alarm lights flashing inside either.

Mac had studied the building blueprints, so he followed her, both of them with stunners in hand, just in case.

All this was storage on the left, adjacent to the garage, with offices up and around a corner.

Mac moved even quieter today than she had in the past. Almost as silent as he did.

That was good.

They turned the corner and went down a short corridor, to where it opened out into an office bullpen, ten desks pushed together in clusters, but only half of them seemingly in use with those little personalizations people accumulate, like pictures of family or little toys.

All the offices around it were dark. That had been a concern, that one of the inner offices they couldn't see from across the way might have had someone working extremely late.

"This way," Mac motioned with her free hand, crossing partway then turning right again.

Rob was a ghost trailing her.

"This is it," she said, touching a door.

Rob nodded for her to go ahead then turned himself sideways to keep watch.

Just in case.

The door wasn't locked. She pulled it open and a chill breeze kissed his cheek.

He waited while she went in and then followed.

Now, things got dicey. An ambulance might roll up with a body to deposit. Supposedly, they all had the codes to access the building at night and knew the procedures to follow.

But they might just appear as the bay door at the far end of the room opened, surprising the hell out of him and Mac.

"Checkpoint three," Mac said next.

"So far, so good," Alicia replied.

She was also monitoring fire emergency channels, where ambulances got called out. Hopefully, nobody else needed to transport a body in the dead of night.

Rob locked the door behind him, just to buy them a few extra seconds in an emergency, then moved to the far end of the room where he had a view of the garage door and the exterior door on the front quad. The well-lit front quad they had so assiduously avoided while getting in here.

Mac sat down at the desk and went to work.

Alicia had given her a small unit to plug into the machine. She did so, then leaned back.

If everything went well, the little thing Alicia had

programmed would walk right up to the computer's brains, introduce itself, and then be invited inside.

Alicia was also monitoring it from the truck, parked about a mile away. She might have to step in, take charge, and beat that same computer mind to death, hopefully before it managed to call for help.

Any alarm would give away the game. Even to a smart person doing records.

Rob couldn't help that his breathing kind of stopped as he waited on tenterhooks for the game to move to the next stage.

"We're in," Alicia said over the line.

Rob let go his breath in a heavy sigh matched by Mac.

Mac started typing. This was where her expertise came into play. She and Alicia knew computer systems everywhere and could make them sit up and dance. Rob was good with people.

"F-2 looks promising," Mac called to him after a few minutes studying the screen.

Rob moved over and looked at his options. Letters across from the left. Numbers from bottom to top.

F-2 was closer to him, middle. He grabbed the handle and pulled.

The faint whiff of cold death he'd been trying to identify earlier got stronger as the drawer opened fully.

Female. Nude. Average to skinny build, which was good. About the right height, which was better. Scars and faded tattoos that spoke of a hard life. Rob checked her arm and found marks where she'd used a hypoinjector to mainline something good directly into her veins.

Every civilization had people who developed problems with consumption. Even when you tried to help, some folks would slip through the cracks. Or squirm their way, unwilling to be told otherwise.

She'd had a rough life, looking at her face. It was drawn and looked ancient, but she had all her teeth. That had been the great fear. *Salonnia* no longer had Helen's dental records to compare with, but any gaps here would cause questions.

She looked ancient and withered though.

"Actual age?" he asked, glancing over.

"Late forties is best estimate," Mac said, rising and moving closer. "Oh, yeah, I see."

As with other things, she'd bring a woman's senses and sensibilities to this, noticing things a guy like Yankov or Montague would miss.

Mac rested a hand on the woman's arm for a moment, as though communing with her ghost and asking permission.

Something.

"She'll do," Mac pronounced after a few moments of silence.

"Could I get a ride?" Rob asked Alicia on the comm.

"Stand by," Alicia said. "We appear to have a vehicle in the vicinity, so it's your lucky night."

Well, yeah, of course there was a truck close. That jabber was in case somebody had managed to overhear the signal. Always in code.

Rob looked around and found a gurney tucked into a corner. He retrieved it and lined it up on the side of the tray.

"Ready?" he asked Mac.

She nodded and grabbed the woman's feet. Rob got his hands under her torso and neck, then lifted and slipped her onto the rolling stretcher.

Pushing the tray closed, he pulled the gurney over towards the door while Mac went back to the computer.

Up until now, everything had been easy. This was when it got complicated.

Folks who came to work tomorrow might remember that F-2 had been occupied, so the computer needed to show that the woman had been retrieved by somebody, without leaving any cues that might cause some office drone to ask questions. Or make phone calls.

None of this worked if they left any burrs to hang on somebody's mind.

Parking the woman's body, Rob moved to the front door and checked it. Fire exit style, so it could be opened from the inside without a key. Hopefully, Mac and Alicia had enough control of the computer systems around here.

He glanced over at her and got a confirming nod, so she was reading his mind. Also good.

Rob cracked the door open enough to smell the night air over chilled death. That scent really got inside your head and did a number.

Industrial mixed with decay. He would need a long shower later to wash everything so he got the smell off.

Headlights approached, entered the circular driveway. Alicia pulled the van around, stopped, then began to back into place.

Once she got close enough, he closed his door and pressed the big red button that activated the chain drive.

The door opened and let warmer, cleaner air in. Plants and animals that were still alive.

Alicia parked and Rob opened the rear of the machine. Alicia came out the back and slipped by him to go help Mac. That part of the operation was more important than this part.

Rob peeked around the edges of the van, but didn't see anybody approaching, so he moved the gurney into position and collapsed the front legs as he pushed it inside.

Rob joined it, pausing again to look through the windshield.

Nothing but night out there.

He had gone shopping today and found himself a chill

box designed for backwoods camping out of a vehicle. Six feet long inside, two wide, two tall. Perfect for more beer than you and a bunch of your buddies ought to be drinking in a single weekend.

He lifted the poor dead woman off the gurney as delicately as he could and moved her to the chiller. It had been on for hours, so she would really be going from one small, cold coffin to another one. Hopefully, she wouldn't mind.

Being dead for several days helped.

Rob said a quick prayer for her soul and to say thank you before closing the lid and moving back to the rear of the van.

"We have to move fast," Mac was standing there, already pulling the gurney as he pushed. "Somebody noticed the bay door opening and called the desk phone just now. Local police are probably headed this way to investigate us."

Rob hadn't heard it, but he'd been paying attention elsewhere.

"You handle the gurney," he said, a snap decision that saw him moving back to the front of the van and climbing into the driver's seat.

"How long?" he called.

Mac repeated it to Alicia. He watched Alicia finish typing and stand up. She started to move this way.

"Override," Mac called, causing Alicia to turn back and unplug their device.

It would never do to have someone figure out what had just happened.

Mac waited for Alicia to get in, then triggered the garage door and jumped over the sensor beam.

As she got the rear doors closed, Rob shifted into drive and took off. Not a dead run flight that might screech the tires. At the same time not waiting around. He'd mapped everything out ahead of time when scouting earlier, but if a cop was coming, there was absolutely no way to tell from which direction.

He headed towards a residential section of town nearby. Blue collar. The sort of place where a panel van like this might be parked along the street because it was somebody's livelihood.

The last thing he needed to do tonight was explain why he had a stolen corpse in his van. The explanations would go from lurid to disgusting and end up with all of them in jail.

Not good.

Rob drove quickly but smoothly, turning corners randomly every few blocks just in case. Eventually, he got back into the more commercial districts. He looked at Alicia in the rear-view mirror.

"Anything?" he asked.

"So far, they seem to be marking it down as a false alarm," she said, looking up from the clamshell computer she'd been monitoring. "Nobody saw us and the building itself is intact."

"At least until somebody finds the fence cut," Mac offered. "How long?"

Rob shrugged.

"If F-2 is off their radar, they might never put all the pieces together," he replied.

"And if she isn't?" Mac asked.

"Then we might have a problem."

33

CARLOTA TOOK A DEEP BREATH AS THE TAXI DEPOSITED her over a few blocks from her destination. She adjusted her satchel over one shoulder and looked around the neighborhood innocently. Downtown. High rises and offices.

And one publishing company.

According to Rob, the building itself was under constant surveillance, but not that closely. They would likely see her enter, but might not realize it was her immediately.

She had gotten Erika's help to strip all the color from her hair. Not much had lasted this long, so what she had naturally was mostly gray and starting to come in fully white.

Carlota caught her reflection in the mirrored surface of a storefront as she walked and did a double-take at the ancient crone who stared back at her. Makeup tricks pushed the other direction had added wrinkles instead of hiding them. Carlota had even added a bit of a hunch to her walk.

Babushka, making her way, rather than sexy secret agent.

She had to trust Erika.

More especially, she had to trust Rob.

It helped that she'd woken up this morning and realized that she really did want to survive. The game that had sounded so awesome and powerful a year ago had turned out to be a death wish writ large, though it had taken her a long time to fully appreciate that.

Carlota had been railing against a galaxy that seemed to be done with her. Why the hell had she decided to help it get rid of her?

But she knew that answer. *The Rage* was real. All the things that had been foisted on her over the years—the decades—because she was a woman in a system built to maintain men.

She'd lost her cool. Her composure. Had fallen prey to that seductive siren call of destruction.

Until she woke up and decided to survive.

Technically losing was acceptable if it gave her more years to enjoy who she might invent herself to be. Not the old woman in the reflection, though she supposed at some point she might just give up on keeping her hair dark and let herself turn into the sexiest grandma in the galaxy.

Erika had certainly managed something similar.

Today, she was dressed in a casual business suit. Slacks and matching tunic blazer in navy, a particular fabric Rob had picked out. Black shirt underneath instead of white, with a ribbon where a man might have worn a tie.

Sensible shoes for running. Even in heels she could move quickly, but the plan today assumed angry men chasing her.

Men.

Rob had managed to seduce her in a way Carlota wouldn't have believed possible a week ago. He had surrounded himself with competent women and then *listened* to them. Some of the arguments she'd participated in, setting this up, had seen Rob on one side and Carlota and Erika on the other, with the younger woman handling communications security siding with her when she spoke.

And Rob had listened. Changed his mind when their take made more sense. Even thrown himself fully into it, rather than sullenly.

She looked forward to the chance to seduce him later. Erika had whispered a few things in her ear over the last four days.

Carlota crossed the last intersection now and made a point to ignore the vehicle at the far corner across with two men seated in front. Or the one fellow at a nearby kiosk, ostensibly buying a newspaper and coffee.

Amateur hour, if they stood out that badly. The first two looked like cops, rather than agents. The other one was a stringer who would need to seriously up his game if he ever wanted to be fully recruited.

Instead, she pushed open the door to the building itself and went inside, starting a timer clock in her head.

Somewhere, the woman who handled electronics would be watching as Carlota vanished from sight and would set Rob and Erika in motion.

How long did she have?

Carlota didn't know, and found that element of uncertainty comforting. Emil Yankov was as dangerous a foe as they came. How soon would somebody call him? How many resources did he have immediately on tap?

Right here was the game. That surge of adrenaline that she'd missed, dying slowly by inches behind a desk. Any fool could move paper around.

Only a field agent could do something like this.

She ignored the elevator and found the staircase. Better to climb steps than be trapped in a small box. She'd gotten lucky that the man holding the pistol to her chest had wanted to seduce her rather than execute her. Carlota had felt his eyes undressing her and smiling at what he found.

She would take him up on that unspoken offer when this was all done.

If she survived something so crazy.

Armand had shown her how to be an agent again. Erika had reminded her how to be sexy. Rob might be the third piece. Being alive.

Carlota emerged from the stairs and found the door for Constanz Books. She'd only ever dealt with him via comm and mailed package, but Carlota had scouted the place once, at the very beginning.

Learning the field of battle.

She entered the office and smiled at the young woman behind the desk.

"May I help you?" she looked up brightly.

"I'd like to talk to Jan," Carlota said.

"I see," the woman nodded, slightly evasively. "And you are?"

"Carlota Rojas," she replied, watching those eyes get big for a moment.

Initially, Carlota had argued to walk in here looking like she had before. Rob had supported her.

Erika, of all people, had put her foot down hard and refused to budge from the old lady peasant routine.

"If you want to be you tomorrow, you can't be you today," she'd said emphatically.

Looking at the receptionist, Carlota could see the image of the ancient crone burning itself into the woman's memory permanently.

"Certainly," the receptionist said brightly. "If you'll have a seat, I'll let him know."

Carlota smiled and moved with aging grace and stiff

joints she didn't feel, marking the legend as a withered woman.

Old, like Montague wanted to tell himself, those nights when her ghost might sneak up and howl obscenities at him when he tried to sleep.

Jan Constanz didn't take long to emerge from the back. He took her in and saw only the makeup and white hair. That much was in his eyes.

He didn't undress her like Rob had. Or Erika. Didn't linger on her curves with questions as to what they felt like. Tasted like.

She was just another crone. A babushka and nothing more.

He blinked several times in a row as he studied her. Like the receptionist, he would tell reporters and police that she looked old and haggard.

"Madam Rojas?" he asked unnecessarily.

Carlota nodded.

"What a surprise!" he exclaimed. "Please, come back to my office and we can chat."

His eyes strayed to the bag she had brought. It was large enough for stacks of paper. Possibly heavy enough as well. What might it contain? Could that be *The Manuscript* itself?

The man hadn't lusted after her body, but she could see it lingering lovingly on the possibility that he might have the whole manuscript in his hands today.

If he was a good boy.

Carlota rose slowly. Painfully. Walked like an old woman, emphasizing that slight hunch with a bit of a limp thrown in.

Misdirection, which was apparently Rob's signature move as an agent for *Lincolnshire*'s Service.

She followed Constanz into and through a maze of gaps between boxes and desks, noting how everyone had stopped working to stare at her.

Carlota wondered which ones had been quietly suborned by Yankov or Montague and would need to find an excuse to call someone right away with the coup of their careers.

Jan Constanz was still a liberal progressive fighting The Man. That was why she'd picked him in the first place, from more than a dozen options here in Bennan. But she could see where the thought of the money had gotten to him.

Too bad. Still, she supposed that he would at least put it to use grinding the gears of the system, rather than having a harem of bimbos or a string of mansions when this was all done.

"What can I do for you, Madam Rojas?" he asked as they got settled.

She had left the door to his office open. The better for the others to hear this conversation.

"I wanted to surprise you, Sri Constanz," Carlota replied in a husky voice, a little ragged with time and age.

Pouring it on, since she wouldn't ever see the man again, either way.

Carlota reached behind her and opened the satchel. She heard his breath catch with a faint gasp, but didn't smile at his predictability.

She pulled out the whole stack and sat it on his deck, then peeled the next chapter off the top, extracted one page with backing details, and put the rest back in her satchel.

"I've already mailed off copies to everyone else, but wanted to deliver yours in person," Carlota said off-handed, as if that wasn't the single stupidest thing she could have done on the entire planet.

Right up there with calling Emil Yankov personally to taunt him and not expecting the man to have the line traced in moments.

"Thank you?" Constanz replied. "What brings you into town?"

"Call it a whim," Carlota offered, sticking to the broad talking points she and Erika had worked out. "We've reached the mid-point of the game, and everyone needed a little break in their routine."

"And the rest of the manuscript?" he asked, still breathless and jarred out of his own pattern of life by her appearance.

"You'll have it in due course," Carlota chuckled. "It would ruin everything if folks didn't have a chance to stop me, after all."

He nodded, and she could see him at a loss for words.

"How is the publishing process proceeding at your end?" she queried.

"Well," he replied, brightening right up. "We have a cover selected, and are working with a graphic designer to do the back and the dust jacket. Since we know how long it is, we will only need a day or so from receiving the final chapter to do a quick copyedit pass and then send it on to the printer."

"Has anyone warned you that they'll blow up your warehouse or anything silly like that?" she asked.

Imperial Intelligence wasn't known for subtlety. *Salonnia* could be worse, except that most of those warehouses would be owned by some Syndicate who would need to be mollified afterwards.

Or at least warned so they could have an insurance fire.

"We've specifically engaged folks outside our usual suppliers," Constanz nodded primly.

As if that would matter, given the explosive nature of this book. Which was exactly why she was mailing copies to so many places.

Only *Salonnia* and the *Fribourg Empire* would have any interest in suppressing it. Others would titter behind polite hands, while perhaps buying excess copies just to drive it onto bestseller lists. She could see smugglers bringing in pallet-loads later for the black market.

Oh yes, Carlota understood how this game was played.

"Excellent," she said, rising stiffly, still in character. "I expect that I might mail off all the copies on the same day for the last chapter, but not use the slow post for yours. I might even just drop it off again. Until then."

Carlota had happened to be facing in the direction of the open door as she said that, so of course she'd had to speak louder, so that Constanz would hear her. As well as everyone else.

She stepped into the open and noted which folks had retreated back into their offices. Who was on a handset, versus who was actually working.

Which folks might be making spare cash on the side as various intelligence agencies slipped bills into their pocket against today.

Carlota moved quicker than the old woman as she made her way back out, exited, and hit the stairwell with a smile nobody else could see.

Somewhere, fires were being lit under various asses.

Angry fires. Pique at being taunted so boldly in broad daylight, when she was certain that most of the watchers were too busy watching each other to have even noticed her down on the street.

Down she went, but exited a rear door onto the alley. Carlota paused to look up and spot the pulley that Rob had used to get into the building the first time, when he'd been uncertain what he would find.

A panel van was parked nearby. The door slid open as she turned that way and Erika smiled at her.

"How are we doing?" Carlota asked as she suddenly sprinted over and jumped in like a much younger woman.

Erika slammed the door behind her and Rob started driving.

"All hell is breaking loose," the younger agent monitoring things said, beaming. "Slowly, though. Inertia is an utter bitch after this long."

"Nobody would believe I'd be dumb enough to do something like this?" Carlota laughed as the van rumbled out the back of the alley and turned into mid-day traffic.

"Professionals are predictable," Erika laughed with her. "The amateurs are the ones that mess everything up. And that was about as amateur a move as we could come up with."

Carlota grabbed a seat and strapped herself in as Rob turned another corner, moving with a sure certainty in his hands and motions that she was certain would translate later into other things.

"Okay, I have the first alert," the younger analyst called. "Police are being summoned and given the old woman description with an all-points notification."

"What about the goons?" Rob called from the front.

"Yankov's people, if they are his, are in a complete tizzy, and talking on a channel that's not encrypted. Low-use channel. Open dialogue. Someone is reading them the riot act."

"Let me hear," Rob ordered.

The woman pulled a headset and the back of the truck was filled with his voice.

"Yes," Carlota said. "That's Yankov."

"Recording this for later?" Rob asked from the front.

"Absolutely."

"Good."

Rob went back to driving and Carlota reached out to take Erika's hand. Who could have imagined that a strange, black box theater filled with an alien musical would lead to all this? More than once in the last few days, she'd wondered if her personal atheism needed to be modified slightly.

Someone, somewhere, seemed to have decided that they liked having her around. *Lincolnshire*'s Service wasn't that powerful, so they had some pull with some entity.

Erika smiled at her, as if reading Carlota's mind.

"Now, the fun starts."

34

———

EMIL WOULD HAVE LIKED TO TAKE A LAYER OF FLESH OFF someone for this, but he was alone in his office. It was an unprepossessing place. Front area for a receptionist he had brought with him from *St. Legier*, an office for him, a pair of conference rooms with maps and pictures, plus a small kitchenette and bathroom in the rear.

Homey, without his people having to be any more exposed to outsiders than necessary. Technically, as Imperial agents, they were supposed to be operating with the cooperation of the locals, but Emil trusted those fools about as far as his old bones could throw them on a good day.

That might have bit him in the ass now.

He slammed the handset of the comm down hard enough that it probably cracked under his hand, but Emil was past caring.

He rose from his desk.

"Conference room!" he roared. "NOW!" and stomped that direction.

Lunch time, so it was him, the young woman who

handled communications and reception, plus only Sergey, who had been doing something instead of having a martini.

"Alert everyone," he said to Sergey. "Get them down there immediately. With descriptions. Start passing out bribes to random passersby. Flash fake badges if you have to. Flood the area and find me something. Go!"

Sergey took off like his tail was on fire.

Emil turned to the young woman. Katherine, though he rarely thought of her in those terms. Young as an agent, but smart. Possibly another *Hummingbird*, another Carlota Rojas, another thirty years down the line when she was no longer pretty but still brilliant until some fool came along and forced her out of the field.

Could he change that?

Doubtful. Karl VII was a well-intentioned man, and Emil had heard good things about the crown prince, but *Fribourg* was far more than those two men. It was a great river that would take generations to change, and Emil suspected that too many people—after he was gone—would draw entirely the wrong lesson from Rojas.

And there was nothing he could do about it.

"You will take charge of all communications," Emil decided, elevating the woman in his own mind, for what little good it might do tomorrow. "Do not wait to contact me with questions. You know the policy as well as I do. Use your best judgment, understanding that speed is more important than accuracy."

"Sir?" she asked in a gaspy, surprised kind of voice.

"A good plan today beats an excellent plan next week," Emil quoted from an ancient admiral whose name he had forgotten. "I will be in the field, trying to chase Rojas down. You will handle everything here. Questions, Katherine?"

She paused for long enough that she was rifling through various scenarios and ideas in her head.

"No, sir," she said after a moment, transforming somewhat into a more confident woman.

He supposed that was also his fault, having had so little interaction with her, though she was trained equal to the man around here, lacking only experience.

Had he screwed up there as well? What might a woman's perspective have given him, in chasing down a much more dangerous woman?

Emil made a note to explore that question much later.

Right now, someone had finally located Rojas. She was either taunting him directly, or had tired of the game and just wanted someone to kill her so she could be done with it.

He would be happy to oblige.

Emil rose and took a step before stopping. He turned back to Katherine.

"Alert local military and gendarme forces," he instructed her. "Use my credentials to inform them that this might turn into a chase, and that she might finally try to escape the planet, having been trapped for so long."

"Their response, sir?" Katherine asked.

"Kill her," Emil said simply, turning back for the door.

35

Rob had been taught combat driving by the Service. How to use a vehicle of this mass and power offensively when needed. Today, it was just traffic hemming him in. That had been the risk, but any earlier or later in the day and it would have been worse.

And a ground vehicle was much easier to hide. *Salonnia* had their share of repulsor-equipped vehicles, but Rob hardly trusted most people moving in two dimensions. Adding a third was generally an invitation for trouble.

He glanced up at the women in back. Alicia was plugged in to every comm channel possible. Mac and Carlota were holding hands and watching.

It was his game.

"Police status?" he asked.

He had to remember not to speak Alicia's name out loud, so he was looking at her in the mirror.

"They're starting to review the same camera footage I've been using for weeks," Alicia said with a grin. "Slower than I expected, but they've found someone who saw Helen emerge from the rear and get into a van. Our description is so generic that I'm tempted to hack in and update it in their records."

Rob laughed. Professionals insulted by the amateur hour happening back there. *Salonnia* had never been a serious threat to anyone, because the Syndicates didn't like the thought of a well-organized, well-run government. They just wanted the kickbacks and grift.

"We can afford to wait at the far end," he reminded her. "I'd rather be too early than too late. We are playing high-stakes poker here."

Carlota reacted to that, but Rob had only gotten snippets of her game that had won her so much money that she'd had to just carry it around in bricks, unable to launder that much by depositing it. Not without questions. Legal, official questions.

He turned down a side street at the first chance, then ducked the van into an alley. They were tight for a vehicle this size, but he had insured it on rental. Always a smart move when somebody might be shooting at you later.

They made better time, even cutting across stalled traffic. Right up until they hit a garbage truck coming the other direction. Neither of them had lifters. Traffic had closed up behind him.

"Mac, out and spot me backing," he ordered, then remembered that he was supposed to call her Erika.

Of course, it wasn't like Mac was her real name either. Just the gun-toting badass chick he hung out with occasionally. The one who taught doctoral-level courses in mathematics and cryptography on the side.

She slammed the door open and started walking aft.

"Comm security?" he asked, eyes alighting on Alicia.

"Chickens minus heads, but there is a young woman on the line currently issuing orders in Yankov's name," Alicia said. "She's got her shit together, too. Expect them to start quartering outward soon."

Crap.

Rob hadn't been counting on Yankov deciding to abandon his home base to take charge in the field, but either option would have hobbled him. Nothing Rob had seen had led him to expect Yankov to hand things off to a woman agent who stayed back while the old man took charge forward.

They weren't screwed, but the walls were going to close faster now.

Mac had gotten far enough and was gesturing for him to back up out of the garbage truck's way. She even slid out into traffic as he got close enough, blocking those folks and giving Rob space.

Then red and blue lights began to flash.

Shit.

At least they were on the ground. A cruiser rolled up to Mac, then cut across two lanes when he realized why she was standing there.

Rob held his breath and motioned the other two women to vanish. It helped that the back of the van had no windows.

His truck beeped as it backed, this time. They'd disabled that for the morgue to reduce the number of people that might have heard, but he was glad that he'd fixed it today. The road back there was open enough for him to emerge from the alley backwards, bump into the street, and crank the wheel over hard to line up with the flow.

The officer emerged from the cruiser and waved at people. Fortunately, he wasn't returning their obscene gestures just yet. Having a beautiful woman standing there probably helped.

Rob had his window down to listen. Just the sounds of

traffic, plus the men and women in the garbage truck working their way forward slowly.

Rob was clear. Mac started to move to get back in, coming around to the passenger door up front.

The cop waved at them, then paused.

Rob saw recognition of the panel van crystallize in the man's eyes.

"Hey, you, wait a minute!" he yelled, still watching Mac's bottom.

It was a fantastic, distracting bottom, in relatively-tight dark blue dungarees, with a gray shirt and a brown leather jacket over that.

Rob dropped the gearbox into reverse, in case he needed to get offensive with this much weight.

They could not be captured like this. It would blow everything, and get Carlota killed. Maybe him, too.

At the least, his usefulness in *Salonnian* or Imperial space would be greatly impeded if someone got his face, voice, and fingerprints on file as a *Lincolnshire* agent.

Not good.

The cop was walking this way, hand only resting on his sidearm. Class four, like Rob preferred, rather than the stunner on his off-hand.

Bad design, but nobody asked Rob. It meant that lethal force was the first choice, rather than the second or third fallback. Of course, they were talking *Salonnian* cops.

Rob had an especially low opinion of those folks, all of it personal.

Mac had paused, but the cop was watching the van. Even made eye contact with Rob.

The only reason that Class Four was still holstered was probably because Mac had been right about Carlota looking old and gray today, instead of mature and smoking hot. She did that, too. Not in Mac's league, but very, *very* few women he'd ever met were.

The cop approached.

Rob was about to do something when Mac turned back to him, stunner suddenly in hand, and shot him dead center in the chest. He went down like a sack of potatoes.

Rob slammed the gearbox to park and exploded out of his door, reaching the downed cop almost as fast as Mac did. Thank whatever gods cared that he'd been alone in his cruiser, rather than having a partner back there drawing and shooting at them.

"Grab his feet," Rob ordered, squatting enough to get the man's shoulders.

They lifted. Rob backed, carrying them to the curb, then setting him down gently enough. He grabbed the man's radio and slid it across the concrete hard enough that it fell into a sewer opening and vanished. Still one in the car, but Rob didn't want to take the time to disable it. That might also sound alarms somewhere.

They had about three minutes before he woke up, minus whatever concerned citizens called the emergency line right now to report what had happened.

"Move," Rob said to Mac, the two of them racing to the van and jumping in.

Traffic had thinned because of the bottleneck, with only one lane getting through until somebody moved that cruiser.

Rob slammed it into gear and gunned it forward.

Someone would figure this out shortly.

36

———

EMIL WANTED TO SCREAM.

He'd had a team in place. They'd watched an old woman enter the building. Even taken pictures of her. Then filed them and gone back to whatever they'd been doing before.

He snarled at the two men.

"Find her, or I will abandon you on this planet when I leave, and strike you from the records as employees when I get home," Emil said carefully, standing next to their vehicle.

There were extra police forces around, which just hindered things, because the cops were a blunt instrument in a delicate situation. Worse, they were backing up traffic every which way. No vehicles could get anywhere.

He needed options.

Emil pulled his comm from his pocket as the two bumbling fools got into motion.

"Rittendorf Imports," Katherine said brightly as she answered.

"It is Yankov," he said glumly. "I need a repulsor equipped vehicle as a personal transport at my location. Do we have any handy or do we need to rent or steal one?"

"I already have a rental vectored in on your location, Agent Yankov," she replied. "ETA ninety seconds. The driver will either remain with the vehicle, or turn it over to you, depending on your immediate needs."

Emil felt his mouth fall open. She'd already seen the need. Understood it. Addressed it. Found a solution. Implemented it before he'd gotten to the need.

What else had he fucked up? Was he too old for this game?

It happened. One day, the skills had atrophied to a level where the mind wasn't capable of reacting fast enough.

Should he just retire when this was all done? Kill Rojas and then go home and call it a career?

"Excellent," he managed to rasp. "Thank you, Katherine."

Emil cut the line and watched others run around, interrogating random citizens and local workers. Some of them he could see were his. Some *Salonnian*. At least two belonged to somebody else, but didn't get close enough to be clearly identified.

This whole intersection was a shitshow unfolding.

A low beeping overhead announced the arrival of a flying car of some sort. There were already two police vehicles grounded, but this was not one. Smaller, for one thing. Two seats at most.

For a moment, Emil considered just taking it and leaving the driver behind, but he was feeling more mortal today, so he approached as it landed in an open parking spot nearby. Emil flashed his own badge to the driver as the man opened the door to exit.

"No, you drive," he instructed the young man.

Young. Emil had been young once. Now, he was feeling those intervening forty years. He settled into the passenger seat.

Two seats. Boot for cargo. Lifters. Not much else. Hopefully fast.

"Lift off and get me above the city," Emil instructed the man, not even bothering to learn his driver's name.

Emil had a badge and enough authority to use it offensively today. And it felt like he would need it.

After the months of chasing Rojas, had she suddenly woken up this morning tired as well? This much done with the whole thing?

Time to go out in a blaze of glory, because tomorrow sounded like too much work?

Emil had grandchildren to spoil and landscapes to paint, but that badge in his pocket suddenly weighed more than the pistol on his hip, both of them anchors threatening to drag him to the bottom of the sea.

Yes. Kill Rojas and go home.

The car lifted off smoothly and was able to climb slowly out until the towers were all below him. The kicked-over anthill didn't look so bad from up here. Distance would do that.

Emil's comm rang. He checked the ID.

Katherine.

"Yankov," he said on answering.

"Maybe nothing, sir," she replied. "But I have a report of a police officer that was attacked with a stunner not far away. Shot by a woman, though her description didn't match Rojas. Dark haired, rather than the gray our agent at Constanz reported. However, the officer thinks he recognized the van as matching a description from your location."

Emil leaned far enough out to see the streets below. The chaos as yet another police vehicle rolled up and two detectives got out. Or politicians. Plainclothes whatever.

"Where?" he asked her. "And the man was not hurt?"

"Stunner, short range," Katherine confirmed. "Then a

male accomplice driver helped move the man out of the street before fleeing. Unconfirmed witness report. About a mile and a half southeast of Constanz Books."

He was clutching at straws, but this was the only straw that hadn't been fool's gold so far.

"Southeast?" he confirmed, gesturing to the driver to head that direction. "Isn't there a small starport southeast?"

"Stand by," Katherine said.

He heard her moving papers around, so she must be in the conference room again. Or still. With all the maps. Smart choice on her part.

Smart woman, and he'd had her answering phones and getting coffee instead of running her in the field like an agent.

More the fool him?

"Affirmative, Agent Yankov," Katherine was back. "Wyland Field. Mostly commercial rather than passenger transport. Also a large number of small JumpSail-equipped starships."

Emil felt his bowels turn cold. They'd been driving away, her and her accomplice. Headed that direction, and stumbled into an officer, who got suspicious. She'd shot him, but only a stunner, because he was just a man doing a job, rather than a deadly threat.

Dark hair? Probably she'd worn a wig to see Constanz, then pulled it off when she got into the van. That would fit. Accomplice explained how she'd been able to elude everyone for so long. Rojas had hired someone to do things for her. Or found an old friend.

Emil had missed him because everyone had been concentrating on Rojas. And he'd not bothered to ask the only woman on his team how she would have done it, were she in Rojas's shoes.

More the fool him.

"Thank you, Katherine," Emil said firmly, understanding how badly he had messed up, but not until Rojas had rubbed his nose in it. He hung up and turned to the driver. "Wyland Field. Now."

The man nodded and concentrated on his flying.

He would see Rojas dead.

37

CARLOTA WATCHED ROB PULL THE VAN UP TO A DISTANT hangar from the main part of the starport. He'd driven like this was a race. In many ways, it was. Hopefully, they had won.

Everyone bailed out of the van as it came to rest and she watched Rob and Erika (Mac?) draw weapons and enter the garage through a small door like they were clearing a building. Again, professional. And had worked together enough to be comfortable covering each other's backs.

There was a touch you only developed after shooting people with someone else. Carlota could testify to that.

She waited by the side of the van as the young woman on comm security monitored things.

"Rob, we've got trouble," she said conversationally, but Carlota knew that he and Erika were wearing earpieces. "I have Yankov vectoring in traffic on our location. Good guess on his part or we were made somewhere."

She paused, then turned to Carlota.

"He wants you inside, now," she said.

Carlota moved quickly, entering the garage as Erika

opened the bay doors beside her. The small starship inside had lines like a courier, rather than a yacht. Needle-prowed and sleek. Just the sort of thing a team of two might fly on either relatively short hops, or an extended vacation which touched every inhabited planet along the way.

Rob was standing inside the hatch, waving her closer. She entered behind him.

Cramped, yes, but well organized. Bridge to her left. Common kitchen in the middle. Cabin just aft, with a door she presumed went to the engine room. Rob had gone forward. She joined him.

Bridge with two seats that you accessed by mostly climbing in between them. Not something for anyone with a belly to do comfortably.

"You sit here," Rob said. "I'm headed aft to set things up. Call Yankov and walk that script, then we move quickly. Remember, he's already headed this way, so we have probably three minutes."

Then he was gone.

Carlota took a calming breath and focused herself. Rob had copied a business card he'd found at Constanz Books. She accessed the comm network and punched in his number.

Emil Yankov. One of the most storied Imperial agents still working. Simply a legend in *Salonnia*. And still in the field, though he was more than a decade older than they'd told her was too much.

For a woman, anyway.

"Rittendorf Imports," a young woman answered the line.

Carlota opened visuals, just because Erika had been right. Carlota in makeup looked old, and the camera on this ship wasn't that good.

"Is Emil about?" Carlota asked. "It's Carlota Rojas."

Again, the gasp, shock rattling the young woman to her very core. Young, too. Maybe twenty-five. Blondish hair that hadn't started coming in gray anywhere yet. Blue-green eyes filled with intelligence and savvy.

"He's in the field," the woman replied. "Would you like to contact him directly, Agent Rojas?"

"No," Carlota shook her head, sticking to the script she and Erika had worked out. "Let him know that I'm done. That I'm tired and I'm leaving and that he's won. You'll never see me again."

She cut the line, then ignored the call back when the youngster tried to engage her in…what? Conversation about what it was like to be hunted by every intelligence agency worth their salt in the galaxy? And a few that weren't?

What it meant to be female, when only men were supposed to be smart and competent?

Carlota could write books about that. Had, but it wouldn't ever be published. It was a shame, on certain levels, but this was a peace offering to Emil, if he would only take it.

She left everything powered on and checked the connections. All good. Everything was powered up and ready for immediate flight. She could run away and never be found again.

But only if Emil Yankov and Imperial Intelligence would allow it.

Noise behind her and Carlota looked. Rob dragging a box on wheels.

"You ready?" he asked.

Carlota rose and nodded.

It was now or never.

38

────────────

EMIL WOULD HAVE LIKED TO COME SCREAMING IN AT tree-top level, sirens howling fit to wake the dead.

That was not an option at a starport. Terminal Operations meant that everybody had to be grounded at least a mile from the fence in every direction, and never rise above thirty feet altitude inside that.

No zipping over the perimeter. Not even for an agent of Imperial Intelligence.

Well, he supposed that he could, but that would require escalating things to the very top. He could probably do that as well, but it would take time.

More time than he had, if Rojas had called Katherine to taunt him.

And that was how he saw it. That or she really had woken up this morning and had enough.

Emil understood that flavor as well. He was feeling his age today.

He was ready to go home and be done.

So they were driving in. The young man had gotten them down in a landing pad specifically for such, then merged into traffic. It helped that this was a commercial field rather than passenger. You could drive reasonably close to your ship to unload things, then park or send the car home.

But he had no idea which ship she might be in. Emil grabbed his comm.

"Rittendorf Imports," Katherine replied instantly.

"Yankov," he said. "I'm at Wyland Field. Let us assume that she's running from here. I need you to contact the authorities and ground all ships. I don't care what story you tell them. Smugglers. Terrorists. Kidnappers. Just get the place locked down hard and start sending police and agents this direction so we can search every vessel and ground vehicle around. She cannot be that much ahead of me, and nobody has taken off in the last thirty minutes."

"On it, sir." And she was gone.

Emil knew that he'd have never even considered issuing such an order to the woman yesterday.

When she'd been a receptionist.

Because he was a fool. In the end, if Rojas got away, nobody would blame him, but Emil would go to his grave always wondering if Katherine could have found her.

If listening to another woman would have been the smarter way to find a woman.

Water under the bridge at this point. He needed to nail Rojas's hide to the wall as a trophy. Kill her if she wouldn't be taken alive, and then go home and retire.

He was done.

"Orders, sir?" the young man driving asked.

"Skip the terminal," Emil said. "Get me into the launch areas. See if you can find a van that matches the description from downtown. If they ran this way, they are boarding a ship to leave, and that means they left the vehicle close by. You have the notes?"

"Yes, sir," he said.

Emil concentrated on the view as the man turned and headed around the main building, down the wide roads where service trucks might rumble.

There were few around today. Mid-day, and few folks were coming or going. That worked in his favor, as the roads themselves were almost empty.

His comm chirped. Katherine.

"Yankov," he said.

"I have the Flight Control Tower on another line," she said quickly. "I have invoked certain authorities that you will need to be aware of, but they are ones that you previously covered in our agent briefings, so I believe that we are on sound legal footing. They have ordered all vehicles grounded. Local military authorities have also gotten involved, as I took the liberty of assuming that gendarme forces lacked the ability to threaten or stop a starship once it left the ground. Should I retract?"

Emil considered everything she'd just said. All of it was exactly correct. Probably sharper than most of the male agents could have repeated. But then, he supposed that Katherine had to be twice as good as any of the men he'd brought, just to be taken half as seriously.

Because she was a woman.

"You have done appropriately, Katherine," Emil said. "Thank you. Please take charge of all of our agents currently in the field and get them routed in this direction. Wyland Field is large, so we will need exceptional personnel reserves in order to search everything."

"Understood, sir," she said.

Emil cut the line and felt old.

Then he saw something out of the corner of his eye. Why it stood out, he couldn't say, but some facet locked him.

"Turn right here," he snapped.

The driver squealed the tires in the process, but got the

vehicle about in time to not crash into anything. Not that Emil cared. Rental, and he had the resources to repair it.

Hell, he could buy it outright from operational petty cash if necessary. They'd already done that with several, just because long-term economics had worked out that way.

"Yes," he muttered.

"What am I looking for?" the driver asked.

Emil pointed.

"Through that gap," he said. "There is a dark blue panel van. That matches the description from the police officer. We'll start there. Are you armed?"

The man looked over at Emil like the older agent might bite him, then Emil realized that the youngster was a civilian, not an agent.

Pity that he hadn't brought Katherine. She was probably a better shot than the others, as well.

Twice as good. Half the respect.

He needed to fix that, though he had no idea how at the moment.

But that was tomorrow. He needed to kill Carlota Rojas today.

The driver was good. They whipped quickly around a curve and turned a corner that got them close. The van was a close-enough match for him. The vector was as well.

He was playing a long-shot, but what else did he have at this point? Rojas had been taunting everyone for months, first by mailing her damnable manuscript everywhere, then by remaining on *Borlait* while the hunters circled.

Until one morning when she'd woken up and it had all weighed too much. Like Emil's day was proceeding.

"Stop here," he ordered, jumping out with a pistol in hand as the car came to a halt.

The van was outside of a small hangar. Inside, he could see the bow of a sleek courier through the open door. That was his first solid clue, as the doors would normally be closed to keep out weather and pedestrians. This ship was preparing to depart, and he'd gotten here in time.

Emil grabbed his comm as he raced up next to the van and jammed his pistol inside the open side door. Another clue. Someone was moving in a hurry and hadn't even shut up their truck in their haste.

"Rittendorf…"

"Katherine, they are in bay 72," Emil overrode her. "Get everyone here immediately, as they have not taken off yet."

Rojas made a liar of him at that moment, however. Emil heard the engines and repulsors power up with a sharp whine that quickly built to a low roar of power.

He moved to the front fender of the truck and aimed, but his pistol could to nothing against a starship.

The craft idled forward at a slow walk as he watched.

Emil got a good look at the front windshield and saw the pilot for just a blink of an eye. White hair was the thing that caught his attention, then the cockpit rotated, rising smoothly.

He fired anyway, mostly out of anger at himself.

To have gotten so close, only to fail at the end.

Still, she could surrender to the authorities as they surrounded her on the flight out. Or she could die.

Either way, Emil Yankov would be packing everything up tomorrow, apologizing to Katherine, and heading home.

The roar turned into a wind as the starship powered up and headed towards the launch ramp. Even then, it was already too high and moving too fast for a proper pilot. Some civilian would get his credentials revoked for flying like that.

Emil figured that Rojas didn't really care all that much.

As he watched, the craft stood on its ass and the engines unleashed a howl of power, driving it smoothly into the sky like an arrow coming off the string.

Had he gotten here in time? Had Katherine?

Would it be enough?

A streak of light out of the east caught his attention. Emil had been blessed with exceptional eyesight as a youth, and it had remained excellent into old age, so he was able to pick out a pair of old Imperial starfighters. A-8, he thought, but Emil would need binoculars to be certain.

Salonnia only received third-line craft, secondhand from Imperial stores. It didn't really matter, though, as the starship that was fleeing was completely unarmed. And had been caught low enough that they could chase her all the way to the edge of space, keeping up with all but the fastest ships.

How fast was that courier?

Emil knew a moment of dread as the three points of light danced in the sky and got higher and higher.

She couldn't outrun them, could she? Had she stolen this particular ship because it had the power/mass ratio to show her tail to starfighters?

Shit.

Did orbital forces have anybody that they could scramble on short notice? Would they take Rojas serious enough to do so?

Would anybody listen to Katherine, even speaking in his name, in time to stop that woman from getting away?

Then a flash of light as a new star appeared briefly in the southern sky. Hopefully, they had waited until her inertia would carry her wreckage outward far enough not to land on any of the resorts, because he recognized that flash for what it was.

The two starfighters had opened fire. Scored a solid hit against a craft with no shields.

Shot Carlota Rojas down.

His comm rang. Katherine.

"They've opened fire," she said simply. "The craft is in freefall."

"Have them watch for parachutes or anything similar," Emil said tiredly. "Then get me the exact coordinates of the crash. Once you have those, buy, rent, or steal a transport and join me at the crash site immediately."

He hung up, but not before he heard her gasp. It was good.

This old dog could still surprise people. Could still learn a new trick.

Could undo some of where he'd gone wrong.

Emil returned to the car and pointed as he climbed in.

"Head that way as soon as we can get clear of the field and in the air," he ordered.

Emil Yankov had to see that Carlota was dead for good this time.

39

CARLOTA LEANED BACK AS ALICIA CUT THE COMM LINE. She'd finally gotten properly introduced to the woman, though she could see why Rob and Mac had waited until now. Carlota might have backed out. Might have fled.

Might have spent the rest of her life looking over her shoulder for men like Emil Yankov to finally catch up with her.

"Now what?" Carlota asked, looking around.

Rob and Mac had a cozy starship, apparently named *Widowmaker*. Alicia had set up a remote control console on the kitchen table, and Rob was flying her stolen ship.

Had been flying. It was freefalling in pieces now. Possibly on fire, as the image on the screen showing the bridge was fuzzy. Smoke? Or internal electrical shorts.

"It slams into the ground in about forty seconds," Rob said matter-of-factly. "The front end catches on fire in a few seconds, burning your corpse beyond recognition, even before the bow hits at terminal velocity and destroys your body."

"Her body," Carlota corrected him automatically. "She

might have already been dead, but between the four of us, her sacrifice will make it possible for me to survive. To escape. And we never learned her name?"

She was facing Erika as she asked that. Mac. Whoever she was.

Carlota's savior in more ways than one.

"We did not," Mac said. "They had her down as an indigent, possibly dead from a narcotic overdose, with no immediate identification papers available. Rob and I have been calling her F-2 for the drawer she was in when we stole her."

"That will never do," Carlota said, turning to all of them. "I propose we call her Carlota, as she took my spot in line for death. I will become Helen. That was how you found me. Saved me."

She reached out a hand and Mac took it, squeezing. And not just Mac. Now-Helen reached and took one of Rob's as well. He'd set things in motion in a way Helen had never really imagined possible, bringing along another Carlota to sniff and track the first one.

Nobody else had assumed a middle-aged woman would be good enough to be a threat. Rob had assumed she was at least his peer and treated her as such.

It was good.

Even Alicia put a hand on Helen's shoulder, perhaps a benediction of rebirth.

"Will they believe?" Helen asked Rob.

He shrugged, but there was a wicked gleam in his eyes.

"The aft section with engines and crew cabin should withstand the crash," he said. "The back half of the manuscript is in a reinforced case that should survive impact and flames. Yankov will get his hands on that and see the other half of the book that will never be published. At least, not until a lot of time has passed."

"Wait," Helen said. "What?"

"Did you leave a copy with your lawyer, with instructions to open the package in the event of your untimely death?" he grinned at her.

"Oh."

"Exactly," Mac said, still holding her hand. "You can be dead, and still reach back from beyond the grave to have your revenge on people."

"But I didn't keep a copy," Helen said.

Alicia laughed heartily.

"Good thing somebody quickly scanned all those remaining pages then, isn't it?" she asked.

Helen watched her pull a memory chip from a pocket and hand it to her.

"This is all of it, except what's already at various publishers," Alicia said. "Plus we have copies here so you can recreate everything when you finally are dead long enough."

"Thank you," Helen said simply.

She couldn't see it from here because *Widowmaker* had no windows in the kitchen on that side, but if she could, the van and the stolen starship's now-empty hangar weren't more than one hundred yards away. Two bays over and across the street, which was why Rob had known about the ship.

That and an appreciation for things that went fast.

Helen—she got to be Helen from now on—watched the screen as her supposed starship continued to tumble, at least from the way the horizon indicator was turning clockwise. She'd never really learned to fly all that well, which was why Rob had been remotely piloting.

But without her personnel records, Montague wouldn't know anything beyond what Emil Yankov told him.

Would it be enough?

"And here we go," Rob said.

Helen watched as fire engulfed the small cockpit. The

blue suit she was wearing was made of the exact same material as the Carlota whom Rob had put into the pilot's chair before they left. The material would burn well. Carlota would be reduced to a charred corpse, then possibly broken apart on impact.

Assuming Yankov found the manuscript, then he could verify that it was her that had died in the crash.

And she would be free.

Helen rose from her seat and leaned over to kiss Mac on the forehead, then wrap her arms around Rob awkwardly and just hug him as hard as she could.

"Thank you," she repeated herself. "I'd hit the end of the road and never realized it. They would have killed me."

"That's on Rob," Mac smiled. "When he asked me to impersonate you, I did the same thing, letting the rage take hold and run rampant for a while. He was the one who asked what my endgame was. Neither Alicia nor I had had one until that moment."

"So what will your superiors demand?" Helen asked the man. "Is Miguel Cabrill still in charge of the Service?"

"He is," Rob nodded. "His was the decision to send us, but he never expected we'd find you. My job was to mostly spend my time identifying all those agents running around looking for you for his files. That includes the young woman at Rittendorf Imports who doesn't show up in any of our files. As to what he wants from you, I presume immediately he wants the rest of the manuscript, so that will buy you time. Then you made out like a bandit at the poker tables, so you won't really need money for a while. That will help. Eventually, they'll want to buy more information off of you, so make sure you don't sell it cheap."

"You could just take me prisoner, you know," Helen pointed out.

"Things done without active, verbal, positive consent just

aren't as much fun," he smiled at her, meanings on a variety of layers far beyond what a man that young should understand.

Somebody had been teaching that boy. And well.

Helen looked forward to final exams sometime soon.

"So you'll haul me to *Ramsey* and turn me loose?" she asked coyly.

"If it were up to me?" Rob asked. "Sure. Miguel will have the final vote. But again, you as a friendly witness and talking is far better than holding you in a cell and threatening you for information. You can never trust something someone tells you under that sort of duress. Eventually, they are just making shit up and hoping you like it."

Helen nodded. Interrogation was all about building rapport with a person over time. Being friendly and drawing them out. Whips and abuse just hardened most people.

You caught more flies with honey than vinegar, as her mother had always said.

The screens had all gone dark. Impact or at least enough fire damage to render all the electronics dead. Carlota Rojas was dead with them.

Good riddance.

Who might Helen be, if she could be anybody she wanted to?

Helen caught Rob's appraising glance and smiled.

Anybody she wanted.

40

___

Emil stood off to one side and watched. Ships like that weren't supposed to catch fire on impact. Safety systems were designed that way.

At the same time, civilian vessels never expected to come under military fire that ruptured things and caused them to fall out of the sky.

At least he had people to do the dirty work. The craft had been falling pretty much straight down on impact, but *pretty much* was still enough to scatter debris, and it had been barely in one piece before hitting.

It was in a few million pieces now.

The fires were out. Fire departments were standing by, but they'd already found Rojas, still strapped into the pilot's seat. Most of her anyway. She'd died in flames, then the bridge had sheared her into two main pieces that medics had removed on two gurneys.

Police kept the perimeter, while Emil had invoked the full depth of his authority and kept everybody else at a distance. Only his people and a few he trusted from *Salonnia*'s Bureau were allowed near the craft.

It was finally cool enough. The sun would be down in another hour.

Katherine emerged and started this way, carrying something in her hands. Of course it would be Katherine. Emil had brought one diamond and a lot of quartz with him.

She was smudged with soot and bleeding from a scratch on her wrist just above her gloves. He could smell the smoke on her clothing and in her hair.

However, the smile on her face was a precious thing. He looked at the satchel she was carrying.

"It's here," she said triumphantly, flipping the top open and handing him a stack of papers.

Chapter Seven greeted him on the top of the first page.

Emil felt his heart stop beating in his chest, then reset so fast that it was racing.

Quickly, he read the first few pages. Then flipped to Chapter Twelve and read that in its entirety, since Rojas had promised to burn Grendel Montague in great and damning detail.

And she did.

Good gods, woman!

Since his team had found Rojas, and chased her down, and killed her, Emil felt a certain possessiveness to the manuscript. The *Salonnian* Intelligence Bureau would get a copy. Eventually. But only a copy. The original would return to *St. Legier* with him.

In fact…

Emil handed it back to Katherine's confused hands.

"You take charge of it," he instructed her, enjoying himself and the hard looks some of the men close enough to hear were giving the two of them. "I want a full writeup, including which agents and operations have been compromised, even if the information never comes out."

"We assume it will?" Katherine asked.

"We do," Emil nodded. "I would have set up a deadman switch somewhere. Somebody nobody can find in time, who has a copy. I expect that all the publishers will get the entire remainder at once. Constanz was ready to start printing in days. So will everyone else."

"I'm not senior enough for this assignment, Agent Yankov," Katherine said boldly, as if daring him to take it away from her again and give it to one of the quartz fools.

"You should be," he said simply. "I was a fool not to see how good you were at the beginning, so this is my way of making it up to you, Katherine. Had I listened to you, we might have caught her. Everyone chasing the woman was male. Do you think any of us could understand what a fifty-three-year-old woman would be thinking?"

Fortunately, she kept her opinions to herself, though Emil was certain he could detect a hint of *I could have told you* in her eyes.

Because nobody thought to ask the only woman on the team.

They shared a nod and he gestured for her to go get some coffee from a stand that the fire department had brought with them to the middle of nowhere. They must have experience in dealing with situations like this.

Emil stared at the shattered wreckage, still smoking in a few places and crawling with his quartz agents. Then he watched his diamond get some coffee, grab a free chair, and start reading.

Carlota Rojas was dead. That much was certain. He could tell his team to pack up tomorrow and they would be home in a less than a week, depending on flight arrangements.

Then he was going to have to remain in harness for at least another year, just so some idiot on *St. Legier* didn't fail to look past Katherine's gender and fail to discover how smart the woman really was.

Carlota had taught Emil a very valuable lesson. One he doubted that anybody from *Salonnian* Intelligence would ever absorb. It was likely that Montague needed to go. Either he retired gracefully or Emil would leak parts of Chapter Twelve and let angry Syndicalists eat him alive.

Either way, he'd be out of the picture. That was good enough for now. Later, Emil would need to find a way that everyone else didn't repeat this egregious mistake.

Katherine would be in this exact, same place in only thirty years.

READ MORE

Be sure to read all of the Handsome Rob Gigs!

Can't Shoot Straight Gang
Can't Shoot Straight Gang Returns
Hunting Handsome Rob
Handsome Rob Assassin
Kinetic Solutions

Available at your favorite retailers!

ABOUT THE AUTHOR

Blaze Ward writes science fiction in the Alexandria Station universe (Jessica Keller, The Science Officer, The Story Road, etc.) as well as several other science fiction universes, such as Star Dragon, the Dominion, and more. He also writes odd bits of high fantasy with swords and orcs. In addition, he is the Editor and Publisher of *Boundary Shock Quarterly Magazine*. You can find out more at his website www.blazeward.com, as well as Facebook, Goodreads, and other places.

Blaze's works are available as ebooks, paper, and audio, and can be found at a variety of online vendors. His newsletter comes out regularly, and you can also follow his blog on his website. He really enjoys interacting with fans, and looks forward to any and all questions—even ones about his books!

Never miss a release!
If you'd like to be notified of new releases, sign up for my newsletter.

http://www.blazeward.com/newsletter/

Buy More!
Did you know that you can buy directly from my website?

https://www.blazeward.com/shop/

Connect with Blaze!

Web: www.blazeward.com
Boundary Shock Quarterly (BSQ):
https://www.boundaryshockquarterly.com/

ABOUT KNOTTED ROAD PRESS

Knotted Road Press fiction specializes in dynamic writing set in mysterious, exotic locations.

Knotted Road Press non–fiction publishes autobiographies, business books, cookbooks, and how–to books with unique voices.

Knotted Road Press creates DRM–free ebooks as well as high–quality print books for readers around the world.

With authors in a variety of genres including literary, poetry, mystery, fantasy, and science fiction, Knotted Road Press has something for everyone.

Knotted Road Press
www.KnottedRoadPress.com